D1585130

H. Alexander

from M. R. K.

Dec 21. 1948

THE CRESSET LIBRARY

GENERAL EDITOR: JOHN HAYWARD

THE ADVENTURES OF BARON MUNCHAUSEN

SINGULAR TRAVELS, CAMPAIGNS
AND ADVENTURES OF

BARON
MUNCHAUSEN

by

R. E. RASPE and Others

★

With an introduction by

JOHN CARSWELL

Illustrated by

LESLIE WOOD

★

LONDON
THE CRESSET PRESS
MCMXLVIII

Published in Great Britain in 1948 by
The Cresset Press Ltd., 11 Fitzroy Square, London W.1
Printed by the Shenval Press, London and Hertford

CONTENTS

CONTENTS

INTRODUCTION

BARON MUNCHAUSEN'S TRAVELS have made no author famous, though they have found their way into a score of languages and to countries which even the Baron himself never visited. They could be condemned as neither distinguished in style nor novel in subject matter; and yet they seem to have struck the common chord of humanity. 'Travellers,' wrote Barnabe Rich, 'are privileged to lie'; and this is surely an important aspect of the wider truth that all men are privileged to romance. The most popular works of travel (or indeed of imagination) from the Odyssey onwards, have been *Voyages Imaginaires*. Like his predecessors in the genre, Munchausen was no ordinary journeyman; his most impressive adventures are those of the mythological hero. The few who have succeeded in bending Ulysses' long bow, have made their attempt from many motives; but whatever these may have been, whether satirical, like Swift's or Lucian's, or instructive, like Defoe's, the author and his purpose seem to be dissolved in the delight of a grateful posterity. For most readers Swift's carefully pointed shafts have lost their poison, and we skip the meditative Crusoe.

The greatest of Defoe's gifts was an artful shading of the products of his imagination into the understood terms of ordinary life. The palate must be accustomed to the rich diet of fantasy. The ingenious interlocking Chinese boxes of the Arabian Nights, by which each narrative is encased in an equally extraordinary, but highly circumstantial explanation, is another method of meeting this need for acclimatization. The circumstances of Munchausen's creation call for at least one such Chinese box. Like Scheherazade, the author of these *Travels* romanced with ruin waiting in the dawn. The story of his arrival in that situation is as strange as Scheherazade's own, and serves both as prelude and contrast to the flights of imagination which arose from it. Rudolf Erich Raspe, a social outcast who suffered from all the incommodities of earthly travel, created a traveller free of all restraints, his own, and the world's emancipated self.

Rudolf Erich Raspe, the undoubted author of Munchausen's narrative, was born in Hanover in 1737, the son of a respectable accountant in the Government Department of Mines. The father, an amateur of fossils and the companion of the mining engineers of the Harz Mountains, had married a Prussian Lady of Junker family, Luisa Catherina von Einem, and it was through her that the influence of two Masonic uncles was brought to bear on her only son. She too, was the inspiration of his romantic faculty. His first romance—'aus den Ritterzeiten'—has as its background the neighbourhood of his mother's family seat.

Raspe's youth was spent in the apparent stagnation of a small German State. In scores of little courts, rococo princelings basked in second-hand glory; in the universities, adjacent to the palaces, the learned of the day revolved in a formal frenchified dance. There were, however, two facts which distinguished Hanover from its neighbours. The double monarchy of George II provided a duct through which English manners flowed to the lesser of the partners and established an ascendency over the French outlook in a land where imitation was the rule. The second fact was the foundation at Göttingen, in the year of Raspe's birth, of the last of the 'ancient' universities of Europe and the future cradle of German Romanticism, by the former Hanoverian Minister in London, Gerlach Adolf von Münchhausen.

Raspe went up to Göttingen when he and the university were both eighteen years old. He was an intelligent, red-haired boy, with an urgent desire to make his mark in the learned world. His pastor, at his confirmation, may have had a deeper insight, or may merely have thought the boy a prig and a bookworm, when he wrote in his pupil's album:

> *Quid iuvat innumeros scire atque evolvere libros,*
> *Si facienda fugis, si fugienda facis?*

If this was the album which Raspe later carried on his travels, he had ample opportunities to ponder this entry.

His parents made heavy sacrifices to send their clever son to the university, and it seems that from the very beginning Raspe was short of money. A year after his matriculation he migrated to Leipzig as companion to a young nobleman named von Lüden, and began to accumulate what he after-wards described as 'debts contracted out of zeal for learning and youthful frivolity'. Under the influence of Johann F. Christ, the aesthete and friend of Lessing, he began to develop an antiquarian and artistic taste at once wide and well-informed; but he was more scientist than aesthete, and better fitted to classify antiques than to appreciate them. More powerful in its sway over his mind was the influence of Leibniz; when, in 1762, as a subordinate in the State Library at Hanover, he published his first work, it took the form of a contribution on Leibniz as a mathematician to the *Nova Acta Eruditorum* of Leipzig.

This was a career so far undistinguished, but promising. He was himself confident of his own talents. In 1763 he published an ambitious work on volcanic geology—*Specimen Historiae Naturalis*, which soon gained him international scientific fame. His development of the principles of Hooke—Raspe already knew English—earned the praise of Sir Charles Lyell eighty years later, when he commented that it was a matter of astonishment that such a 'luminous exposition should for more than another half century have excited so little interest'. Less spectacular, but more potent in its ultimate effects on his own and succeeding generations, was Raspe's other production this year, a purely literary venture. This was a dissertation on the allegedly Ossianic poems published a few months previously in London by Macpherson. Raspe, whose sharp eyes ranged far in his search for material on which to employ his talents, was not slow to see that here was a happy hunting ground for the stirring romantics. His article in the *Hannoverscher Magazin*, which included copious translations, was one of the first arches of the great Gothic revival in Germany.

Such versatility began now to be seriously noticed. He was dubbed '*puer septem artium*', and taken up by the pundits of the University. He responded with all the devotion of the ambitious man in an age of patronage. No poet, he hastened to improve his chances of preferment with a one-act romance in honour of Queen Charlotte's birthday. His publication of Leibniz's posthumous papers brought him before the public with the honour of having edited the papers of the most distinguished German of the preceding generation. He was now secretary of the State Library, and soon found a distinguished patron in General Walmoden, the illegitimate son of George II and Lady Yarmouth, and owner of the largest artistic collection in the Electorate. The learned and energetic librarian was delighted with a commission to catalogue the military aesthete's galleries and cabinets. His life began to expand. He attended masquerades and balls with the 'beautiful and agreeable wife' of his cousin, von Einem, who bided his revenge; he joined the circle of admirers that courted the opera singer, Elizabeth Schmeling-Mara, and was permitted by her to interline the Italian of her scores with a more easily understandable German translation. Borne on a rising tide, he allowed himself the luxury of strident polemic, and attacked his critics both publicly and privately with a caustic wit which, though it was designed to please his patrons, earned him little affection even among those who agreed with him. A particular target of Raspe's indiscreet sallies was Christian Adolf Klotz, a critic disagreeably strict, who had lately migrated from Göttingen to its rival Halle, whence he propounded a rival aesthetic theory. With all the confidence of utter egocentricity, Raspe discharged against Klotz a splenetic cascade; this victim also bided his time.

For the moment all was going well. The idol he served above all others, his international scientific reputation, continued to prosper. He was introduced to Benjamin Franklin, then making a European tour, was deeply impressed, and spent the spare time of the next few months devising improvements to Franklin's glass harmonica. In 1766 he published *Hermin und Gunilde*, a chivalric allegory dedicated to his mother, which has claimed the title of the 'Erste Romanze der Deutschen'; another unsuccessful suitor of Elizabeth Schmeling-Mara lampooned it, but it is otherwise forgotten. A more important contribution to the Romantic revival was his introduction of Percy's *Reliques* to the German public in a long article published in the same year. Supreme good fortune was now at hand. In August 1767, by the interest of Count Walmoden, 'the trusty and well-beloved Rudolph Erich Raspe' was appointed Councillor, Professor of Antiquity and Keeper of the Collections to Frederick II, Landgrave of Hesse-Cassel.

Lessing described Cassel about this time as 'une des villes les plus belles et les plus agréables de toute l'Allemagne'. Its ruler, the Landgrave, was a vacant, if ambitious man who enjoyed light opera and the flattery of a small court. He was married to George II's daughter, Mary, and moved politically in the orbit of the House of Hanover. 'I daresay,' wrote Horace Walpole, 'that in his own country he is reckoned very lively, for though he don't talk much, he opens his mouth very often'; but then Walpole was no lover of his country's German connections. As became a man of rank, the Landgrave maintained a large collection of miscellaneous antiques; how large he did not quite know, for the elderly Swede who had acted as curator for the past twenty years had never prepared a catalogue. The Collegium Carolinum, Cassel's university, was in the same way more ornamental than useful; professors outnumbered pupils. Raspe's combined salary as Professor and Curator was modest, but sufficient for the tepid academic life it was intended to support.

The new Curator saw his preferment not as a haven, but as an opportunity. From the moment of his arrival at Cassel his activity and energy in every direction disturbed the sleepy little court. His brain hummed with projects. With ingenuous enthusiasm he surveyed, catalogued and rearranged the Landgrave's collections, discovering in the process some six hundred hitherto unlisted items. Every piece that could be found was dutifully included in the twelve volume 'Catalogus Perpetuus', which he presented personally to the Landgrave. He took this opportunity to ask for an advance of capital, to clear himself of creditors who grew daily more vociferous. His European reputation was costing him more than a tenth of his salary in postage alone, and he owed about three years' income to moneylenders. But he told only half the truth, and for his zeal as curator—Herder (who much admired Raspe and who borrowed his copy of Percy's *Reliques*—one of the most influential recorded loans in literary history) commented on the readiness with which he displayed the collections to chance visitors—he was rewarded with the additional salary of a post in the library. His energy did not slacken. He was member of the Government Committee on agriculture; he translated Algarotti's then popular text book on Architecture, Painting and Music, and did not neglect his feud with Klotz, who kept up the campaign. In his own hand he engrossed fresh statutes for the Collegium Carolinum, and sent prospectuses far and wide to his European acquaintance, broaching his 'Plan of Liberal Education, in Arts, Languishes, Sciences and Morals' (so he expressed it in a letter to the Rev. Sidney Swinney, F.R.S.) 'which young nobles and gentlemen . . . may have at Cassel to a better rate . . . than somewhere else'. Most other universities, he added, were 'more calculated for scholastic pedantry, or French dam'ed gallantry'.

The same letter to Swinney began with effusive thanks for 'Reccommandation to the eldest as well as to the most distinguished litterary body', a proposal for Raspe's election to the Royal Society of London having in fact been drawn up very shortly after his preferment to Cassel. Raspe had long sought the honour, and had cultivated any distinguished Englishman who came within range—Sir John Pringle, the surgeon, and Colonel Faucitt, the military envoy, with more even than his usual assiduity. For his ambition was westward turned; in his day-dreams he saw himself tutor to the Prince of Wales, and one of the leaders in the new scientific approach to nature. 'Ich sah die natürliche Geschichte nicht als ein Spielwerk an, wie manes bis dahin in Hessen gethan hatte. Sie ist Kenntnis der natürlichen Reichtümer.' It was in England that the exploitation of natural riches by science was already in train. On June 1st, 1769, he was elected a fellow of the Royal Society. At the end of the month Raspe wrote to his friend Nicolai rejoicing in the 'entirely unsolicited honour'.

A new edition of the *Specimen Historiae Naturalis* had been part of the campaign that had carried him into the 'eldest as well as the most distinguished litterary body'. Learned works, however, might bring honour, but they brought few rix-thalers, and it was for want of these that Raspe, in his hour of success, was in the greatest of difficulties. He applied to the Prime Minister of Hesse for assistance, and received only soothing answers; further promotion might some day be possible, if the Landgrave were caught at a favourable moment; there were fees to be made in the reformed Colle-gium; in the meantime, a young vigorous man of thirty-three, with his career before him, should be able to make a profitable marriage. Raspe shrank from explaining the full precariousness of his position; he withdrew, and hoped for better days.

Pupils did not flock to the Collegium, and despite Raspe's deferential suggestion that His Serene Highness should found a Kunsthistorisches Museum illustrative of German Art through the Ages, the Landgrave evidently felt that he had bestowed as much on learning as became a prince, and re-warded the actors in his court theatre with more than double the salaries of his professors. Only marriage was left; and

Raspe chose as his bride a girl of eighteen, half Prussian, half Huguenot, Elizabeth Langens, daughter of a wealthy Berlin doctor. When the ceremony was over Raspe was the richer by 2,000 rixthalers. His credit and spirits temporarily revived.

This assistance came, alas, too late. To satisfy his pressing creditors—mainly moneylenders, who threatened him with a bankruptcy that would ruin his European reputation—he was already deep in what he later described as 'a labyrinth from which there seemed no escape'. His attempts to draw himself out by blurting half truths about his 'miseries and embarrassments' to the authorities, brought no relief. With a naïve resolution he plunged into fresh projects. He had high hopes of the results of his investigations into the natural history of Hesse, published in 1774, but the Government was less interested in the possibilities of Hessian mineral wealth than in the export of Hessian subjects to fight for George III. They fobbed him off with a 'mediocre increase in salary' of 200 rixthalers, less than a tenth of what he owed. In collaboration with Jacob Mauvillon, a physiocrat and military historian of Huguenot origin, he began in 1772 to publish a chatty periodical called the *Casselische Zuschauer;* it reached its twenty-fourth number, and collapsed. In doles and loans he raised 2,000 rixthalers from his father-in-law; but neither to his family nor to his superiors had he the courage to admit the whole truth—that since 1770 he had been embezzling the medals committed to his charge.

Whether or not Raspe's enemies suspected the true situation, this was the moment they chose for their literary counterattack. Under the Aristophanic motto 'Brekekekex', they published an anonymous series of scurrilous lampoons entitled *Neuen Kriegslieder* dedicated to Raspe, and ridiculing the literary circle surrounding Herder, Lessing and Merck, of which he was the most vulnerable member. 'Zu Hannover Raspius tota cantabitur urbe,' wrote the delighted Jacobi to Klotz, celebrating their success. Raspe's reaction was characteristic. He did not retract, neither did he fight back; he wrote instead a long appeal to Gleim, the mentor of Jacobi, denouncing the attack as unfair, and begging him to use his influence to restrain his disciples. Although in 1772 death removed the insatiable Klotz, there were others no less formidable ready to step into the gap thus formed in the ranks of his enemies. Among them was the crippled mathematician, Lichtenberg, who was to deliver the last and deadly blow to Raspe's self-esteem.

In 1774 a last opening in the gathering gloom of Raspe's life seemed to offer a way of escape. Previous applications to be allowed to visit Italy on the pretext of buying for the Landgrave's collection (but in fact to raise money in a market where he was not known) had failed, and he had had to spend his vacations at Clausthal in the Harz, among his father's mining friends. But now it was suggested that he should go as Hessian Resident in Venice. The salary was not much larger, but the prospects of further promotion were good. He accepted with enthusiasm. Securing a substantial advance on account of travelling expenses which he threw to the creditors who swarmed with renewed fury at the news of his impending departure, he set out for Berlin with the ostensible object of lodging his wife and her two children with her parents, and the real one of borrowing a very large sum from his father-in-law. For there was one snag in the Venetian project; what was to happen when he handed over the keys of the collection to his successor?

Dr Langens, told as much of the truth as seemed safe, advanced a thousand rixthalers against his son-in-law's prospects. It was not enough, and even if it had been, it came too late. On November 14th, 1774, arrived a summons to return to Cassel; loath to part with them, Raspe had sent the keys of the collection to his assistant from a post-house on the road to Berlin, with the observation that pressure of work had prevented him handing them over formally before leaving the capital. The authorities now demanded that he should be present at the taking of a formal inventory. He returned. It must have been a dismal Christmas. Still struggling to avoid the public bankruptcy, 'which I have always considered the meanest and most contemptible of expedients', he silenced the last of his creditors with his father-in-law's loan. Then, from the very Catalogus Perpetuus which he had himself compiled, Raspe's fraud was exposed. He confessed at last in the most abject terms, vainly implored the Prime Minister to help him, and on March 15th fled from Hessian territory to Clausthal, the mining village in the forest. Thence he wrote beseeching forgiveness from the Landgrave, and intercession from his friends at court. He threw himself on the protection of the Duke of Brunswick, in whose territory Clausthal lay. But, as he commented afterwards, 'It would perhaps have made a better impression on the Prince, had I not fled'. However that may have been, the Landgrave did not now hesitate. 'Councillor Raspe, born at Hanover, of middle height, face long rather than round, small eyes, nose somewhat large, beaky and pointed, red hair under a short stumpy periwig, wearing a red coat with gold facings . . . walks, in general, hastily', was posted as a fugitive from justice throughout North Germany.

Waiting at the post-house, he saw the warrant among the mail which arrived on March 19th, and considered burning it. But again his courage failed him (he explained later that he had refrained out of consideration for his friend the post-master). Betrayed by the loquacity of his servant, he was placed under arrest while the formalities of extradition began. Three days later, with the probable connivance of the local authorities, he escaped from custody and left Germany for ever, leaving no indication of his route save a Polish seventy-ducat gold piece—one of the finest specimens of the Land-grave's collection—which was recovered by the police from a pawnbroker in Hamburg.

From the safety of Holland he wrote his apologia full of self-pity and ingenious special pleading, which, when it was published two years later, can only have served to revive the flagging animosity of the Landgrave. His pay, he explained, had long been in arrears. He had chosen medals for the pawn-broker with the utmost discrimination, taking only those which lacked aesthetic or antiquarian interest. Such remarks are in themselves enough to explain why it was that other scandals, more damaging financially and more brazen in execution, were forgotten, while Raspe's name was remem-bered in Hesse to the end of the century as shameful. His enemies hastened to destroy what was left of his reputation. His cousin, von Einem, suggested that paste had been sub-stituted for the Landgrave's collection of jewelry, an accusa-tion found to be untrue; others alleged that he had framed Statutes of the Collegium with the sole object of preserving his personal hold over the collections; his very knowledge of Latin was impugned.

At this distance of time his letters show the inward contortions of the natural victim, eternally thwarted of what he calls his 'Hopes' of international scientific fame. For a moment, in the morass of misrepresentation and excuse too naïve to be called disingenuous, emerges the real man—'My hopes had a basis in my inner conviction that I was fulfilling my fate, and doing honour to the service of my Prince; . . . they took their source from the graciousness of the Landgrave, the benevolence of the minister, and from the friendship and goodwill . . . of the learned abroad. Here was no dream of stiff-necked self-love; in all the circumstances it[1] was stark reality.'

From the moment he disappeared on the night of March 22nd, 1775, Raspe lived in the shadows. While he was pouring out his indiscreet self-justifications from Holland, and complaining that the belongings he had had to leave behind him were worth far more than the sum he had embezzled, the Hessian police were in fact cataloguing his possessions, for the Landgrave was determined to recover what he could. There, on the shelf where Raspe kept his work-books, standing beside Percy's *Reliques*, Lessing's *Versuch vom Alter der Ölmahlerei*, the scurrilous *Neuen Kriegslieder*, and six prospectuses for his translation of Algarotti, they found two numbers of a skittish and improper Berlin periodical, the *Vade Mecum für Lustige Leute*. These contained, among other unsigned contributions, certain essays in the fantastic of a kind which had long been popular in Germany—the preposterous lie. From all the circumstances it seems likely that these were from Raspe's own pen. The thorough-going police even impounded his Italian bronze of Priapus for the Landgrave's galleries. In the autumn of 1775, with a few grubby papers in his bag, and little else that could be called an asset, their quarry

[1] i.e. The disgrace that would accompany bankruptcy.

disembarked in England, for so long the land of his aspirations.

He began at once to make the rounds of his colleagues in the Royal Society; what story he told them we can only guess, but the truth soon overtook him. On September 27th, as he was climbing the stairs to a reception, he met his old acquaintance, the stooping Lichtenberg. 'He could scarcely speak,' Lichtenberg reported, 'his clothes are not what they were, and he looks almost like . . . like what he is.' Two months later Sir John Pringle, President of the Royal Society, was anxiously seeking confirmation of rumours concerning Raspe's past, from the Hessian envoy in London, Captain von Kutzleben. The envoy's efforts to stave off open scandal in order to give time to make arrangements for extradition were a failure. Two days later, while the Secretary of State was patiently explaining to von Kutzleben that extradition in such a case was legally impossible, but hinting that 'private arrangements' (kidnapping in other words) would meet with no objection on his part, Raspe was ejected from the Royal Society by a substantial majority.

His 'Hopes' were now blighted indeed; but for the rest of his career he showed a courage which in the days of his better fortune he had conspicuously lacked. From his obscurity he still succeeds in convincing us that he was a man of real scientific ability. He was the master of several languages, and in English particularly attained a pungency and idiomatic vigour which shows the pains he had taken to perfect it since he wrote of 'Sciences, Morals and Languishes' in 1769. Even on the vote for his ejection—a process then, as since, almost unique in the history of the Royal Society—he had a small body of supporters, influenced less by sympathy, one suspects, than by political opposition to Court influence in general (George III was said to be very indignant, and to have expressed clear wishes on the subject to the President), and in particular to the Hessian Subsidy Treaty. By the remote patronage of these opposition Whigs, he clung to the outskirts of society for many years. To his patrons, caustic stories about his former employer, and perhaps something more serious about Hessian state business, lent spice to an otherwise disreputable acquaintance.

At first he tried to re-establish his reputation as a scientist with a work on German volcanoes and two translations of geological works obtained from still surviving connexions on the Continent. German was still a language little cultivated in England, and Ferber's *Travels in Italy*, and Born's *Travels in the Bannat* had a real value to the English scientific public. The 'learned translator' was congratulated in the Reviews on his good English and his 'curious and entertaining prefaces'. Through Bährdt, the editor of the *Heidesheimer Korrespondenz*, he succeeded in publishing the apology written in Holland. If after this anything further were wanted to harden the Landgrave's heart, it was the malevolent notes which Raspe contributed to his translation into German of Nathaniel Halhed's masterpiece, *The Lawbooks of the Gentoos*, published in Hamburg in 1778.

Raspe was now well enough established as a learned hack and wit to be received in certain literary circles. Robert Hinchliffe, Bishop of Peterborough and a prominent member of the Opposition in the House of Lords, and Dr Lort, Mrs Thrale's Cambridge friend, took a liking to him, and, much to the disgust of Cole, the antiquary, who followed Raspe's career with a disagreeable interest, they gave him the entrée to Trinity College Combination Room. His Cambridge visits were probably the happiest incidents of his English career. It is true that there were unpleasant moments—an angry professor had him turned out of his favourite coffee-house as unfit for decent society; and the University Librarian watched him narrowly as he experimented with the pigments of the mummy cases and transcribed manuscripts.

It was these manuscripts that enabled him, on his return to London, to approach Horace Walpole with the idea of a work on the origins of oil painting. Walpole, who cannot but have known the whole story, broached the subject with care in writing to the Rev James Mason: 'There is a Dutch scavant come over' (Raspe was a German, and had been in the country for six years) '. . . who has made a discovery in my way.' He goes on to describe the MS discoveries in Cambridge, and concludes, 'Raspe writes English much above ill, and speaks it as readily as French . . . he is poor, and I shall try to get subscriptions to enable him to print his work, which is sensible, clear, and unpretending'. The scheme seems to have broken down, and a few months later Walpole abandoned the struggle—'Poor Raspe is arrested by his tailor, I have sent him a little money, and he hopes to recover his liberty, but I question whether he will be able to struggle on here'.

This was in effect a sentence of social death. For a year or two he struggled on in London, earning a few guineas and considerable contumely for translations of Lessing's *Nathan the Wise* and *Tabby in Elysium*, a mock heroic poem by a former friend at Cassel, Zachariae. The *Critical Essay on Oil Painting* did indeed appear, and a handsome volume it made; but it was Walpole who saw it through the press, even though Raspe's name remained on the title page with his motto:

In nova fert animus mutatas dicere formas.

Now that the last doors of the oligarchic society to which he was accustomed were closed against him, Raspe the man of science turned towards the rising sun of industrialism in the person of Matthew Boulton, the 'iron chieftain' of Boswell, and James Watt's partner. Boulton was the architect of Birmingham's greatness, and is perhaps the most impressive figure among the first generation of industrial entrepreneurs. Liberal in politics, grandiose in his conception of commerce, he was among the founders of the Lunar Society of Birmingham, which included in its membership more able and effective scientists than the Royal Society itself. In pursuit of his intention to 'sell steam engines to all the world', Boulton was in the latter part of the seventies engaged on the modernization of the ancient Cornish tin industry, which had for so long been a privileged enclave with a semi-feudal constitution. By the time of Raspe's final break with Walpole, Cornwall was thoroughly permeated with the machinery, capital, and agents of the firm of Boulton and Watt. From them an agent with high qualifications of skill could expect a certain latitude on the score of character. Matthew Boulton knew well enough how to protect himself.

The thirty letters from Raspe to Boulton which still exist show Raspe already installed as master of an assay office of Boulton's founding, at Entral, near Camborne, in the North Cornish tin belt. There, among the suspicious mining community, the German exile spent the better part of four years. No wonder the Prussian Legation found him hard to trace in his remote village, when they came to serve divorce papers on him in 1785. In his poky office he experimented, prospected, and wrote reports. By his brisk witty manner, by his very oddity, he pierced the traditional barriers which the Cornish miners interposed between themselves and the 'foreigner'. He learned their jargon, and showed them that he knew as much and more about practical mining than they did themselves. More than fifty years later the queer Mr Raspe was still re-membered at Camborne. For him indeed they were no strangers, as they were even to their own countrymen, but reproductions of the friends of his own boyhood, the miners of the Harz forest.

Though he was now a practical scientist, he did not neglect letters. The few guineas he could earn by his pen might allow him at least to cut a gentlemanly figure in a small country town, and be received at the neighbouring seats of Sir Francis Basset and Sir John St. Aubyn. Through his Continental correspondents—these formed one of his most attractive assets from Boulton's point of view—he advertised a *Reise durch England* which was probably never published, for no copies are known to exist, and transmitted a scientific paper to St. Petersburg, where it was duly read at the Academy. The drollery and curious learning of the ex-freemason (he had been expelled from his lodge soon after the scandal) charmed the romantic Sir John, himself an enthusiast in masonry. These were however mere tentacles vainly waving towards the solid ground of re-establishment. For the few guineas he had often before had recourse to his common-place books and his dog-eared library, and now Smith an Oxford printer seemed to fancy a few of his best anecdotes, built round a half-remembered figure of his youth, Hieron-

ymus von Munchausen, the veteran cuirassier of Bodenwerder.

Raspe must have enjoyed writing about Munchausen. It
was the work, one can imagine, of a few summer evenings,
and is charged with that light-hearted malevolence with
which the author revenged himself on the world. There is
more than a merely accidental contrast between Munchausen,
the fabulously successful man of action, and Raspe, the seedy
failure; between the Baron who strikes his hearers into dumb
amazement, and the learned courtier who had never quite
been able to make himself heard at all. The conscious intention was satire, aimed at the enemies who had, as he persuaded himself, ruined his career; but more obscurely the
Baron was the creation of his own inflated ego, and the real
villain of his tragedy. The better part of humanity is after all
condemned to day-dreams of greatness. It is appropriate that
the light-fingered antiquary should be the creator of the heavy
dragoon.

*　　*　　*

The quest for the author of *Munchausen's Travels* is now
mainly a matter of history. Their anonymity, desirable to
support the fiction that the *Travels* represent the Baron's own
narrative, was essential to their satirical, and often libellous
content. Not only Raspe himself, but his contemporary,
Gottfried August Bürger, his friend Kästner, and his enemy
Lichtenberg, have at different times been canvassed with some
assurance as having been originally responsible. Southey in
his *Omniana* even derived the *Travels* from the Portuguese
on the strength of a superficial similarity of folk tradition.
Southey, indeed, or any other who traces the subject-matter

of Munchausen's stories, must be struck by the fact that they belong, for the most part, to the common tradition of humanity which can be fathered on no name. If the origins were composite, so was the development, and many hands have embroidered and expanded the well-nigh inexhaustible theme. An assessment of the parts played by these various pens and influences is further complicated by the odd bilingual character of the work. It is neither original composition nor translation in either English or German. Although it first appeared in anything like its present form in English, it is in Germany that its sources, both immediate and remote, must be sought. In all this fog of origin and jungle of development, however, the figure of Munchausen himself stands out as the indisputable created entity. The first credit for authorship must, therefore, belong to the creator of the hero.

Baron Munchausen first took his place on the world stage in a forty-two page pamphlet published by Smith at Oxford late in 1785 under the title *Baron Munchausen's Narrative of his Marvellous Travels and Campaigns in Russia*. Though there is no surviving copy bearing the imprint 1785, the fact of its notice in the December number of the *Critical Review* for that year puts the date beyond doubt. The romantic poet, Bürger, who had promptly translated it into German with elaborations of his own, neither accepted nor disclaimed authorship of the original during his lifetime; but in 1824 his biographer, Karl von Rheinhart, was at pains to repudiate a work which, he considered, reflected on his hero's seriousness of mind, and explicitly asserted that Raspe was the author, and Bürger merely the translator. Rheinhart's testimony, made to save the author of poems now little read, from the odium of having anonymously written a best seller, might perhaps be con-

sidered partial. He also lays himself open to suspicion by a
minor misstatement of bibliographical fact. There is, however,
more direct evidence that Raspe was the author of the core of
the Munchausen cycle.

Other than Raspe, there were very few men in the England
of 1785 fitted by talents and temperament to write the work
published at Oxford. He had known Gerlach Adolf von
Münchhausen, and had probably met his cousin, Hieronymus,
the retired cuirassier of Bodenwerder, which lies midway
between Raspe's two poles of Hanover and Cassel. To Raspe,
too, the name of Munchausen deserved the ridicule earned by
those who had frustrated his 'Hopes'; and further, he knew
that some popularity could be gained in England by satirizing
things German. The pointed reference to Gerlach Adolf in
the Preface thus becomes at once intelligible.

The racy staccato, which is the Baron's distinctive style,
bears a strong resemblance to the weapon which Raspe used
against his enemies in his acknowledged works. Other touches,
too, though not all of them in keeping with the baronial
character, are yet typical of the tatterdemalion scientist. 'One
effect of the frost,' declares the Baron, 'which I then observed,
is rather an object for philosophical speculation.' The excellent
English (and Raspe's letters to Boulton show with what ease
and confidence he wrote in his adopted language) is occa-
sionally broken by the untranslated proper name, the circum-
locution, or the slightly misplaced idiom which betray the
foreigner, however expert. Raspe's endpiece, the national
anthem of his adopted country, was too much for the solidly
English editor of the Third Edition, who deleted it; but again
it is characteristic of a man for whom no flattery, however
patent, could be indiscreet. One can trace the hand of the

assay master of Camborne in three further touches. The last of which appears to put the seal of certainty on his claim to authorship. The notion that the 'evening hymn' played by the frozen horn may originally have come to the exile from the mining chapel close to his lodgings may be fanciful; but unless there were some special reason for it, Cornwall would seem an odd place from which to begin the ballooning expedition described in a later chapter. Lastly we have the testimony of Mr Jory Henwood that it was probably Raspe who, from his German mining experience, introduced the improvement in technique known as 'stoping' to the Cornish mines. 'Stopes' or steps enabled several miners to work the same face simultaneously, one above the other. Here must be the origin of the otherwise incomprehensible 'slopes' by which Munchausen dug himself out of his hole 'nine fathoms *under grass*', a term by which Cornish miners alone describe the more usual 'underground'.

The fact of Raspe's authorship of the 1785 English edition having once been established and with it, of the Baron as a character, the search for the sources of his subject-matter diminishes from literary to merely bibliographical interest. Even the existence in the issues of the Berlin *Vade Mecum für Lustige Leute* for 1781 and 1783 of two unsigned contributions which give the bare bones of the first seventeen anecdotes can detract little from Raspe's claim to original creation. The two articles, headed respectively 'M—H—NSCHE GESCHICHTEN' and 'NOCH ZWEI M— LÜGEN', are little more than a series of disconnected hâbleries, without more than the most superficial attempt to establish a personality for the narrator. What does seem certain however, is that Raspe had these articles, *or something very like them*, before him when he wrote, for the

English edition reproduces much of their phraseology. Dr Erich Ebstein, in his commentary to the 1925 edition of Bürger's Munchausen, supposed, on grounds necessarily slender, that Bürger was the author of the *Vade Mecum* anecdotes. It seems unlikely that Bürger, if he had in fact sketched his own Munchausen in 1781, would go to the trouble of rendering an English embroidery of it back into German five years later; and equally improbable that a penurious exile in Cornwall would have had access to an ephemeral publication from Berlin. His own notebooks seem a more likely source; and if for the Oxford edition, why not for the *Vade Mecum* anecdotes also? Issues of it were found among his work books at Cassel, and we know that he published on the Continent long after his disgrace. But even admitting that there is more presumption than evidence that Raspe was in fact the author of these earliest known Munchausen stories, so slight a precursor does little to diminish his title to the creation of the hero himself.

The owner of the hero's name, Hieronymus Karl Friederich, Freiherr von Munchausen, was a younger son of the so-called 'Black Line' of the noble house of Rinteln-Bodenwerder in Brunswick. A man of sixty-five when Raspe introduced him to the world, he had long been in retirement at Bodenwerder, where he lived the life of a hospitable country gentleman. In his youth, like many other German noblemen of the time, he had been in the Russian service, as a follower of Prince Anton Ulrich of Brunswick, the nephew in law of the Tsarina Anna. As a cornet in the Brunswick Regiment, Munchausen served against the Turks in the campaigns fought by Count Munich between 1738 and 1740, and was present at the capture of Oczakov which marked the turning point of the war. On November 27th, 1740, he received a commission as Lieutenant. Its signature must have been one of the last acts of Anna's reign. On her death began the crisis which ended with the eclipse of the German interest at St Petersburg, and sent its supporters temporarily either to Siberia, or homewards to Germany. All these events may be followed in the narrative which Raspe composed. Oczakov was in fact taken by a cavalry charge in which Munchausen's regiment took part; and the Baron's rueful comment on the peace of Belgrade, in which French diplomacy deprived Russian military achievement of its just reward, may well have been taken verbatim. The narrative ends with the Baron riding westwards.[1]

Munchausen in fact saw further service. In 1750 the Empress Elizabeth promoted him Captain, and ten years later, when he was only forty, he retired to his estates on the Weser. There he hunted and entertained, becoming known in the neighbourhood for his generosity and graphic conversation. His vein of humour, which has found many modern imitators, was the serious narration of palpable absurdities. One of his guests observed that he spoke 'cavalierly, indeed with military emphasis, yet without any concession to the whimsicality of the man of the world; describing his adventures as one would incidents which were in the natural course of events'. Towards the end of his life the Baron's peaceful and harmless round was violently interrupted by his sudden elevation to the status of a legend. It is given to few men involuntarily to become fabulous while still alive. Munchausen grew embittered and

---

[1] These events may be followed on pp. 18-22 of the first part of the narrative—the Oczakov 'incident' of 1790-91 must have given a fillip of topicality to later editions.

morose. Too self-conscious to continue it, he abandoned the straight-faced humour with which he had once held his dinner-table in helpless laughter. He remarried at the age of seventy-four in an attempt to gain some consolation in a Bodenwerder from which his faithful huntsman, Rösemeyer, in vain tried to exclude the sightseers; but his new wife is reported to have been a hussy, who had her eye on the old squire's estate. The once genial raconteur died in 1797, an unhappy man.[1]

Beyond the real baron in the hierarchy of origins lie what must be the jottings of a lifetime of miscellaneous reading. Raspe had a wide range, and a capacious memory. For general inspiration he relied on the long tradition of *Lügendichtungen* that flowed from late mediaeval Germany. From the monasteries, where monk and vagus had long amused themselves with the composition of *facetiae* or drolleries with which to make seclusion or pilgrimage more palatable, descended a similar and sometimes mingling stream. To the first tradition belong such cycles as *The Six Sillies*, *The Men of Gotham*, or *Scharaffenland*, where the biggest liar was king. From such a tale—the Serbian story of *The Biggest Liar in the World*—comes the story of Munchausen and the beanstalk. Collections of this kind had always been popular in Germany, and the two previous centuries had each produced its 'Munchausen'—the sixteenth *Der Finkenritter* attributed to Fritz von Lauterbach, and the seventeenth Christian Reuter's *Schelmuffsky*. Anthologies of monkish anecdotes provided the matter rather than the manner of Raspe's work. *Facetiae Bebelianae* (published at

---

[1] While it is perhaps Raspe's gravest crime so to have ruined the happiness of the defenceless Munchausen, a far heavier burden must lie on the shoulders of Bürger, who, through his translation, gave the book its popularity in Germany.

Strasbourg in 1508) contains the stories of St Hubert's Stag and the adventure in the fish's belly as well as the account of the horse amputated by the portcullis; but the first two at least are as old as the *Mabinogion* and the Old Testament. The music of the frozen horn is to be found in Castiglione's *Cortegiano*, which appeared in 1528. Many of Bebel's stories found their way into the collection of preposterous anecdotes grouped under the heading of 'Mendacia Ridicula' in J. P. Lange's *Deliciae Academicae* published at Heilbronn in 1664. Over all or any of these Raspe may have browsed. To combine his gleanings with some of the Baron's own sporting adventures, heard perhaps twenty years before at a dinner party at Bodenwerder, and to embellish both with fantasies of his own devising, must have seemed an easy way of earning a few guineas to a man accustomed to laborious and unprofitable work. In the process he left on his hero the imprint of his own disreputable and egocentric genius.

★　　　★　　　★

By the time the Baron was in his grave, his heroic namesake had reached the public in three countries. The overgrowth which sprawled over succeeding editions is unable to obscure or spoil the laconic vigour of Raspe's core.[1] When, in the spring of 1786 the printers contemplated a new and enlarged edition, it seems probable that Raspe was asked to provide further stories; and if it were not for the explicit statement in the 'Preface to the Fourth Edition' that 'the first edition contained no more than was written by Baron

---

[1] A fuller explanation of these developments will be found in the bibliography.

Munchausen', and that the remainder was the 'production of another pen written in the Baron's manner', it would be natural to assume that this was the case. By the time this pre-face appeared, however, the work had already passed to another publisher, and altogether out of Raspe's hands. The distinction between the homogeneous *Travels in Russia* and the more random *Sea Adventures* was clear enough, and it is probable that the editor of the fourth edition inquired no farther into origins. However this may be some traces of Raspe's Baron linger in the *Sea Adventures* and vanish finally only in the continuations proper. The *Sea Adventures* are free of the specifically English topicalities which are characteristic of the later narrative, and, as has already been mentioned, the Cornish starting point of the *French Natural Philosopher* may well be significant. The edition in which these adventures first appear—the third—survives in the library of Göttingen, Raspe's native university, where it must have arrived soon after publication, for it was on this version that Bürger's first German translation was based.

The appearance of another Baron, de Tott, in this section, was intended to provide a foil rather than a victim for Munchausen. A malicious and garbled account of de Tott's origin dates from the fourth edition which made him and not Munchausen's supporter, the illegitimate offspring of the oyster woman and Pope Clement XIV. François de Tott,[1] whose highly popular memoirs were translated into English in 1785, was an enterprising French hussar who had spent his career in Asia Minor and the Crimea in the Turkish service. His father had actually taken part on the Turkish side in the

[1] Lived 1733-1793. The Memoirs were entitled *Voyages parmi les Turcs et les Tartares.*

campaigns of 1738–40, and de Tott himself, even down to the detail of his being light cavalry as against Munchausen's heavy, might fairly be considered as the Baron's natural counterpart. His account of his own adventures, though startling, was substantially true, and it was not at him but at the Roman Church that the episode was originally pointed.

This new edition reached Germany by the summer, and Bürger's translation, bearing the false imprint of 'London', appeared from Dieterich's press at Leipzig in the autumn. The four plates, signed 'Munchausen pinxit' (they may have been Raspe's own work), which had adorned the English edition, were reversed in the copying, and two others were cut as illustrations of Bürger's embellishments; for, influenced by the rising tide of interest in folk-lore, he had clumsily inserted into an otherwise close translation the legend of *The Six Wonderful Servants*. From Bürger onwards, no editor seems to have been able to resist the temptation to add fresh exploits and revise the old ones.

The new edition went more briskly than the first two, and Smith, a small man, now disappeared in favour of a larger firm, that of Kearsley,[1] once the publishers of Wilkes' *North Briton*. The results of this change in proprietorship are fatally obvious in the next edition, published by Kearsley and his London hacks in June, 1786. They gave it the new title *Gulliver Revived*, and added a series of topical episodes ridiculing among others Lord Mulgrave,[2] the polar explorer, and

---

[1] Kearsley had had an interest in the book from the first, and it is worthy of notice that Kearsley and Smith both published from the same address—46 Fleet Street.

[2] Constantine John Phipps, Lord Mulgrave, 1744–1792. He sailed on a voyage to the Arctic in 1773. Published a journal of his voyage 1774.

the balloonists Blanchard and Lunardi.[1] For Munchausen at war they drew heavily on Drinkwater's *Siege of Gibraltar*, which had been published in 1784. There is some excuse for Munchausen's presence at the siege, as there was a substantial contingent of foreign volunteers in the garrison, including Leonetti, Paoli's nephew, with a contingent of Corsicans.

Interference and elaboration were powerless to stay the book's popularity. Kearsley's hacks—we can distinguish three or four different hands—carried their work to completion through four successive editions. In an effort to live up to the printer's advertisement that it 'could fairly be considered as a new work' each was accompanied by additional crude copperplates. Chapter headings replaced the old 'Heads of the Established Facts' for the first time in the fourth edition. For additional matter the syndicate drew on the chatty *Travels in Sicily* of Patrick Brydone, with its musings on the Temple of Vulcan at the summit of Etna, and playful nicknaming of a surly Sicilian guide as a 'Cyclops'. The Travels of Captain Hamilton exhausted this search for topicalities, and for their last chapter the hacks were reduced to a plagiary of Lucian so shameless that in their preface they were constrained to acknowledge it.

These editions, though amusing enough, mark the beginning of the narrative's degeneration. More damaging than the sequels, however, was an extensive revision of what had previously appeared. Not only were germanisms corrected, or, more usually, glossed; hyperbole was heightened, and the rugged edges of the Baron's style planed and sandpapered

[1] The years 1784 and 1785 brought a short-lived craze for ballooning to this country from France. Blanchard crossed the channel in a balloon in 1784 (being the first man to do so by air), and Lunardi made the first aerial ascent from English soil in the same year.

away to produce an imitation of the augustan journalese of the late eighteenth century. Terms which had flowed naturally from the lips of a sportsman and soldier were replaced by the colourless vocabulary of the general reader. The voice from heaven no longer spoke with a sporting oath; the Baron's 'and that I had', became 'and in this I was gratified'; 'great was' becomes 'it was not easy to conceive', and 'I felt exceedingly cold' is dandified into 'I felt the severity of the air'. Unfortunately for the world it is this garbled and gelded text which has been followed by almost all reprints down to and including the Navarre Society's edition of 1930.

From Göttingen Bürger had been watching edition after edition falling into the hands of an eager public, and with the collaboration of Lichtenberg and Dieterich he now translated the latest English edition, explaining in his preface that the additions made since 1786 deserved a wider circulation. At this point the English and German Munchausens part company. By that time there was a French Munchausen also. The firm of Royez had produced a translation in 1787, duly amended to suit the censorship of the tottering Ancien Regime. For their sixth edition Kearsley's exhausted syndicate were driven back for inspiration on Sinbad the Sailor; the *Flight on an Eagle's Back* was the result. To suit the age which was producing *Goody Two-Shoes* and *Sandford and Merton*, the new and edifying title of *The Vice of Lying Properly Exposed* completed what was now launched as *Volume I of The Baron's Travels*.

This was necessary, as Volume II was already on the market. Taking advantage of the doctrine that there is no copyright in ideas, another printing-house, that of H. D. Symonds, had made use of the figure of Munchausen in the campaign against the veracious but almost incredible narrative of James Bruce, the Abyssinian explorer.[1] The points which most offended the incredulous—the eating of raw meat, the deferential attitude of savage to white man—are all underlined; and with them is mingled a mass of allusion to contemporary literature and politics, much of which is neither traceable nor worth tracing. This author, however, unlike the contributors to Volume I, was no patchworker; he had a vivid if erratic imagination, and in surrounding his hero with a body of fantastic and inconsequential characters—Hilaro Frosticos, the Lady Fragrantia, and the aged Marquis de Bellecourt—he anticipated the style which has given us Captain Foulenough and Mr Justice Cocklecarrot, or indeed, Colonel Chinstrap and the Diver. This evasive fantasy, which is drawn out to an excessive length, has only a few memorable moments. Probably the best of them are a brilliant pastiche of Sterne,[2] which contains precisely the right mixture of smut and pathos, with neither explicit; and, appropriately for a work begun by Raspe, but in all probability written in ignorance of his existence, an heroic passage in the Ossianic manner.

Since then the Munchausen extravaganza has reached

---

[1] James Bruce (1730–1794) was one of the first and among the greatest of the explorers of the African land mass. A Scot and a friend of Buffon, he was by nature unsuited to the tepid travelling demanded by the wine trade, in which his family had placed him. After mortally wounding his man in a duel, he took up an adventurous career in Near Eastern politics and exploration which carried him on his famous expedition to Abyssinia and the source of the Blue Nile (which he was the first European to reach). Although his report of these travels was undoubtedly based on facts, it drew ridicule and incredulity on its appearance in 1790: on at least one occasion Bruce defended his good faith by calling a critic out, and it is to this habit that we owe the Baron's challenging dedication to the second part of these Travels.

[2] *Cf.* pp. 96–7.

almost every country, and most nurseries, of the world. Before the eighteenth century was out three volumes of continuation in German appeared at Stendhal, and the Baron at Walcheren and in the Peninsula provided for a fresh crop of topicalities from London in 1811. The cult of Munchausen in Germany was honoured by Immermann in his eponymous novel of 1841, and by Adolf Ellissen who in 1846 wrote an elaborate rendering entitled *Munchausens Lügenabenteuer*. The French romantics also fell under the charm, and Théophile Gautier was responsible for a liberally expanded French version in 1862, which was illustrated by Gustave Doré. The Baron has since appeared in almost every European language, including Esperanto and Erse.[1] The number of editions which has appeared in English alone must run into hundreds.

The crude copper-plates of the old editions long survived, but the continuation of 1811 gave Rowlandson the privilege of being the first great artist to enter this illustrator's paradise. He provided nine coloured illustrations for this edition, which also contained four contributions from the twenty-year-old brothers George and Robert Cruikshank. Forty-seven years afterwards George Cruikshank executed a second series. In the meanwhile Crowquill had designed vignettes for the edition of 1859. German reprints were equally well adorned. Theodor Hosemann in 1839, and Martin Disteli, the Swiss, in 1841 portrayed Barons who still find reproduction on the continent. The genius of Gustave Doré, which was most at home with the more than life size, produced grandiose fantasies such as might be expected from the illustrator of Balzac

[1] The more exotic languages provide *Bard de Máux* (Magyar), *El Conde de las Maravillas* (Spanish), etc.

and Rabelais; with Munchausen, Doré could scarcely have failed to evoke his best. After the high romantics, the nineties in their turn gave Munchausen a new form, with yellow cover and illustrations by William Strang and J. B. Clarke which show the pervasive influence of Beardsley. What shape a Picasso or a Dali would give the Baron, we can only guess; the twentieth century has had to wait till now to give its interpretation of the perennial narrative.

For nine years, from obscure lodging-houses in many parts of the United Kingdom, Raspe was able to watch his Baron marching to increased popularity by ever greater strides; yet he never called to his aid the triumphant spirit which he had himself brought into existence. By no means a modest man, he confined his acknowledged output to such unremunerative works as Born's *New Process*, of which he observed in a prospectus that it was 'not a work for booksellers to speculate upon, nor likely to be read generally'. While it is true that to establish a claim, once *Munchausen* had changed owners and been extensively revised, would have been difficult, the real reason for this strange reticence is to be found in Raspe's own character. He still believed that success of the kind he craved— scientific fame—would some day be within his grasp. 'Les beaux esprits se rencontrent' he wrote to Boulton, who, when Raspe visited him a little later, avoided having so disreputable a guest in the house, by paying instead for his lodging at the local inn. To fulfil the vain hope of mixing with the learned of the age on a footing of equality, it was necessary to preserve the rags of a reputation which he could not bring himself to believe was lost for ever. He had ruined himself in an attempt to avoid disgrace; one cannot be surprised that he rejected notoriety in the hope of fame. His own best interests were, as always, obscured by a strange mixture of professional pride and extravagant self-deception.

Soon after writing *Munchausen* he left Entral and the 'luxury of fire, smoke, and acids' for London. The Cornish tin industry, inflated by Boulton's attempts to build up a cartel, had entered on a depression. Raspe now became an industrial and scientific free-lance. From lodgings in Air Street he acted as scout and industrial counter-spy for Boulton's enterprises. The Prussian Minister of Trade came on a visit, largely of espionage, to this country; 'Beware of Baron Stein' was the melodramatic opening for Raspe's bulletin to Boulton.

The Birmingham firm were not his only employers. James Tassie, the modeller, whose impressions of antique gems were among the first cheap reproductions to reach an awakening public, provided him with work on a massive catalogue which was published after five years' labour, in 1791. It contained an account of more than 15,000 gems in parallel texts of French and English, and is a monument of curious learning. To Tassie also, we are indebted for a medallion portrait of Raspe which is still preserved in the National Gallery of Scotland. Of this the sitter was childishly proud, though in it the unflattering traits noted by the Hessian police, can clearly be distinguished.

Raspe was growing old and lame. He had to take strong doses of laudanum to suppress the headaches which afflicted him every day from 9 till 5. 'That surely will make the devil sleep' was his comment, 'but will it expel him?' Somehow he kept his head above water, doing research for John Nichols, editor of the *Gentleman's Magazine*, and undertaking a mineralogical tour of Western Scotland with a subsidy from the

Highland Society. Of one of the projects arising from this tour, he had high hopes. His notion was the exploitation of the barren domains of the Duke of Argyll, and a company, 'The Argyll Marble Company', was actually formed for the purpose. Bronze tokens for the payment of quarrymen were ordered from Boulton's firm. 'If it did not argue more vanity than I am possessed of,' wrote Raspe in ordering them, 'I could almost wish to have them marked with my own anonymous brazen face.'

While there is much in these twilight doings that is uncertain, or even underhand, there is no evidence that Raspe ever again pursued a career of calculated fraud, such as that which has been alleged against him on no better authority than a paragraph in *Chambers' Book of Days*. It is said that he ingratiated himself with the benevolent statistician, Sir John Sinclair of Ulbster; and that playing a part comparable to that of Herman Dousterswivel in Scott's *Antiquary*, he misled the baronet about the mineral possibilities of his estates and decamped with a substantial advance. On his tour he certainly met Sir John in Caithness. They would have had much to talk about, including Ossian, of whose authenticity the laird was a convinced champion. The tradition of Raspe's odd personality may even have lasted long enough—he seems to have made an impression wherever he went—for Scott to work fragments of it into a novel. But Raspe himself was received in Edinburgh after his tour, with the acclamation of the Highland Society (of which Sir John was a prominent member), and continued for some years afterwards to live there and in London undisturbed.

The Argyll Marble Company went the way of all his schemes. The marble-laden fleet, which he had seen in imagination discharging its precious cargo in the Pool of London, never sailed. Offers of polished marble tables to Boulton were curtly marked 'Rasp' by the man of business, and, un-answered, joined the rest of the humbly jocose correspondence in the file.

In the autumn of 1793, 'Mr Raspe, 10 per 100 worse than yesterday' set out on his last journey. His 'locomotive powers' may have been failing, though he was only fifty-six, but his 'hopes', his fertility of projection, his immense capacity for deceiving himself, were as vigorous as ever. Coal in western Ireland might succeed, where marble in Iona had failed. The 'Erkenntnis der natürlichen Reichtümer' to which he had devoted his life would surely in the end reward its disciple, and he would sit in the Lunar Society yet if never again in the Royal. He was spared another disappointment, for scarlet fever carried him off at Muckross, in coalless western Donegal in the spring of 1794. Before he passes into final darkness we catch one glimpse of this stumbling, lonely, but talented figure, fawning still, but with a jauntiness which had its roots in a profound consciousness of his intelligence and abilities. 'I hope to have very soon the pleasure to wait on you,' he wrote from Dublin, a month or two before his death, 'and to find you and yours and Mr Watt's family in good health and spirits. Then more of fair Hibernia and something also for our polite neighbours the French and their Philosophists. But in particular the sincere respects of your most humble and obedient servant, R. E. Raspe.'

Enough has already been said to show that the text of *Munchausen's Travels*, as usually reprinted, is the product of a long tradition of haphazard revision and improvisation.

Restoration has been undertaken only sporadically, where it has been undertaken at all. Even professedly authoritative reprints such as those of Seccombe in 1895, and Harvey Darton in 1930, have uncritically followed the depraved text of late editions, in the process depriving Raspe of his due and the reader of any awareness of where one hand begins and another finishes. Seccombe's introduction is a model of exuberant vigour, but errs in matters of detail, particularly over the stages by which *Munchausen* reached its final state, and in the narrative of Raspe's life.

The text is here arranged with the twin object of preserving the continuity of the narrative while using the earliest text available for each portion of it. The chapter headings, which have disfigured all editions since the fourth, but for which there is no earlier warrant, and most of the facetious asides inserted by later commentators, have been suppressed in the first four of the five sections into which the work is here divided. The fifth, which is the work of one hand, and was published separately as *Volume II of The Baron's Travels,* appears as it was orginally subdivided when first published in 1792.

It has thus been possible to include the whole Munchausen 'Canon' (i.e. all that appeared before the end of the eighteenth century) and at the same time to reprint in the first and second sections the unrevised Raspe–Smith text for the first time since 1786.

The text for the first section—*Marvellous Travels and Campaigns in Russia*—is taken from the British Museum copy of the first edition of 1785 ('1786'); that of the *Sea Adventures,* from the Bodleian copy of the 'Third' edition (1786), no copy of the second edition, in which the subject-matter first appeared, being available. Here any influence of Raspe ends, and the rest of the work of Kearsley's Grub Street syndicate has been grouped under the two further headings of *Further Singular Adventures* and *Travels in Sicily, the Americas and the South Seas*. For the last section the original title has been used.

In a work of this kind, elaborate explanatory notes would be out of place, though the temptation to provide explanations of the bristling topicalities is strong. But to do so would be to write the social history of a decade; for one of Munchausen's principal aims was to provide a gossip column for his age. The more studious reader can pursue the eddies on the surface of the later eighteenth century to his heart's content, in the Baron's pages. I have however tried to guide him in brief footnotes to the minimum of information that would give zest to the narrative itself, while avoiding recondite ephemera or the officious explanation of references which any informed reader can very well appreciate for himself.

Many collectors have provided me with bibliographical material for my study of the early editions of *Munchausen*, and I have thought it proper to acknowledge this help more particularly in the bibliography itself. In tracing Raspe himself I am in debt to many correspondents for suggesting lines of research and for confirming surmises; but I must particularly record my gratitude to Mr Arthur Westwood, the Assay Master, and the wardens of the Birmingham Assay Office for allowing me to examine and to quote from Raspe's correspondence with Matthew Boulton, which is preserved in the Assay Office Library.

JOHN CARSWELL

PREFACE TO THE FIRST EDITION

Baron Munnikhouson, or Munchausen, of Boden-weder, near Hameln on the Weser, belongs to the noble family of that name, which gave to the king's German dominions the late prime minister, and several other public characters, equally right and illustrious. He is a man of great original humour; and having found that prejudiced minds cannot be reasoned into common sense, and that bold assertors are very apt to bully and speak their audience out of it; he never argues with either of them, but adroitly turns the conversation upon indifferent topicks, and then tells a story of his travels, campaigns, and sporting adventures, in a manner peculiar to himself, and well calculated to awaken and shame the common sense of those who have lost sight of it by prejudice or habit.

As this method has been often attended with good success, we beg leave to lay some of his stories before the Public, and humbly request those who shall find them rather extravagant and bordering upon the marvellous, which will require but a very moderate share of common sense, to exercise the same upon every occurrence of life, and chiefly upon our English politicks, in which *old habits* and *bold assertions*, set off *by eloquent speeches*, and supported by *constitutional mobs, associations, volunteers*, and *foreign influence*, have of late, we apprehend, but too successfully turned our brains, and made us the laughing-stock of Europe, and of France, and Holland in particular.

ADVERTISEMENT TO THE SECOND EDITION

The rapid demand for the first edition of this little pamphlet is the proof that the Public have seen its moral tendency in the proper light. This little collection, which is considerably enriched by the Baron's Naval, or Sea Adventures, is also embellished with views from his own pencil.

APRIL 20, 1786

TO THE PUBLIC

Having heard, for the first time, that my adventures have been doubted, and looked upon as jokes, I feel bound to come forward and vindicate my character *for veracity*, by paying three shillings at the Mansion House of this great city for the affidavits hereto appended.

This I have been forced into in regard of my own honour, although I have retired for many years from public and private life; and I hope that this, my last edition, will place me in a proper light with my readers.

AT THE CITY OF LONDON, ENGLAND

We, the undersigned, as true believers in the *profit*, do most solemnly affirm, that all the adventures of our friend Baron Munchausen, in whatever country they may *lie*, are positive and simple facts. *And*, as we have been believed, whose adventures are tenfold more wonderful, *so* do we hope all true believers will give him their full faith and credence.

GULLIVER   X
SINBAD   X
ALADDIN   X

Sworn at the Mansion House
9th Nov. last in the absence
of the Lord Mayor.
JOHN (*the Porter*).

SINGULAR   TRAVELS,   CAMPAIGNS   AND
ADVENTURES OF BARON MUNCHAUSEN

I

MARVELLOUS TRAVELS AND CAMPAIGNS
IN RUSSIA

I set off from home on my journey to Russia, in the midst of winter, from a just notion that frost and snow must of course mend the roads, which every traveller had described, as uncommonly bad through the northern parts of Germany, Poland, Courland, and Livonia. I went on horseback, which, provided mare and rider are in order, is the most convenient manner of travelling. I was but lightly cloathed, of this, I felt the inconvenience, the more I advanced north-east. What must not a poor old man have suffered in that severe weather and climate, whom I saw on a bleak common, in Poland, lying on the road, helpless, shivering, and hardly having wherewithall to cover his nakedness.

I pitied the poor soul. Though I felt exceedingly cold myself, I threw my mantle over him and immediately I heard a

7

voice from the heavens, blessing me for that piece of charity, saying,

'I'll be damned my son if I do not reward it in time.'

I went on: night and darkness overtook me. No village was to be seen. The country was covered with snow, and I was unacquainted with the roads.

Tired I alighted at last, and fastened my horse to something of a pointed stump of a tree, which appeared above the snow. For the sake of safety I took my pistols under my arm, and lay down in the snow, not far off, where I slept so soundly, that I did not open my eyes till it was full day light. Great was my astonishment now, to find myself in the midst of a village, lying in the church-yard. Nor was my horse to be seen, but I heard him soon after neigh, somewhere above me. On looking upwards I beheld him tied and hanging to the weather-cock of the steeple. Matters were now very plain to me: The village had been covered with snow that night; a sudden change of weather had taken place; I had sunk down to the church-yard whilst asleep, gently, and in the same proportion as the snow had melted away, and what in the dark I had taken to be a stump of a little tree appearing above the snow, to which I had tied my horse, proved to have been the cross or weather-cock of the steeple.

Without long consideration I took one of my pistols, shot off the halter, brought down the horse and proceeded on my journey.

8

He carried me well—yet advancing into Russia, where travelling on horseback is rather unfashionable in winter, I submitted, as I always do, to the custom of the country, took a single horse sledge, and drove briskly on towards St Petersburgh. I do not exactly recollect whether it was in Esthland or Jugemanland, but I remember that in the midst of a dreary forest, somewhere thereabouts, I spied a terrible wolf making after me, with all the speed of ravenous winter hunger. He soon overtook me. There was no possibility of escape. Mechanically I laid myself down flat in the sledge, and let my horse run for our safety. What I apprehended, and hardly hoped or expected happened immediately after. The wolf did not mind me in the least, but took a leap over me, and falling furiously on the horse, begun instantly to tear and devour the hind part of the poor animal, which ran the faster for his pain and terror. Thus unnoticed and safe myself, I lifted my head slily up, and with horror I beheld that the wolf ate and broke his way into the horse's body. It was not long before he had fairly forced himself into it; then I took my advantage, fell upon him with the but end of my whip. This unexpected attack in his rear frightened him much; he leaped forward with all his might; the horse's carcase dropt to the ground; but in his place the wolf was in the harness, and I, on my part whipping him continually, we both arrived, in full career, safe at St Petersburgh, contrary to our respective expectations, and very much to the astonishment of the beholders.

I shall not tire you Gentlemen with the politicks, arts, sciences, and history of this magnificent metropolis of Russia; nor trouble you with the various intrigues, and pleasing adven-

9

tures I had in the politer circles of that country, where the lady of the house always receives the visitor with a dram and a salute. I shall confine myself rather to the greater and nobler objects of your attention, to horses and dogs, of which I have always been as fond as you are, to foxes, wolves and bears, of which and other game Russia abounds more than any other part of the world, and to such sport, manly exercises, and feats of gallantry and activity as make and show the gentleman, better than musty Greek or Latin, or all the perfume, finery and capers of French wits or hair dressers.

It was some time before I could obtain my commission in the army, and for several months I was perfectly at liberty to sport away my time and money in the most Gentleman-like manner. You may easily imagine, that I spent much of both, out of town, with such gallant fellows, as knew how to make the most of an open uninclosed forest country. It is a pleasing remembrance, both for the variety of sport it afforded, and for the remarkable success I met with in pursuit of the same.

One morning I saw through the windows of my bed-room, that a large pond, not far off, was, as it were covered with wild ducks. In an instant I took my gun from the corner, run down stairs, and out in such a hurry, that imprudently I struck my face against the door post. Fire, light, and sparks, flew out of my eyes, but it did not prevent my intention. I soon came within shot, when leveling my piece, I observed to my sorrow, that even the flint had sprung from the cock, by the violence of the shock I had just received. There was no time to be lost. I presently remembered the effect it had had upon my eyes, therefore opened the pan, leveled my piece against the wild fowls, and my fist against one of my eyes. A hearty blow drew sparks again, the shot went off, and I had five brace of ducks, four widgeons and a couple of teals. Presence of mind is the soul of manly exercises. If soldiers and sailors owe to it many of their lucky escapes, hunters and sportsmen are not less beholden to it for many of their successes. In a noble forest party in Russia, I met a fine black fox, whose valuable skin it would have been a pity to tear by ball or shot. Reynard stood close to a tree. In a twinkling I took out my ball, and placed a good spike nail in its room, fired and hit him so cleverly, that I nailed his brush fast to the tree. I now went up to him, took out my hanger, gave him a cross cut over the face, laid hold of my whip and fairly flogged him out of his fine skin, a pleasure and wonder to behold!

Chance and good luck often correct our mistakes: of this I had a singular instance soon after, when in the depth of a forest I saw a wild pig and sow running close behind each other. My ball had missed them, yet the foremost pig only run away, and the sow stood motionless as fixed to the ground. On examining into the matter I found the latter one to be an old sow, blind with age, which had taken hold of her pig's tail, in order to be led along by filial duty. My ball having passed between the two, had cut this leading string, of which the old sow was still chewing the remainder; and as her former guide did not draw her on any longer, she had stopt of course; I therefore laid hold of the remaining end of the pig's tail, and led the old beast home without any further trouble on my part, and without any reluctance or apprehension on the part of the helpless old animal.

Terrible these wild sows are, but more fierce and dangerous are the boars, one of which I had once the misfortune to meet in a forest unprepared for attack or defence. I retired behind an oak tree, just when the furious animal levelled a side cut at me, with such force, that his tusks pierced through the tree, by which means he could neither repeat the blow or retire.— Ho! ho! thought I, I shall soon have you now—sure enough, —and immediately I laid hold of a stone, wherewith I hammered and bent his tusks in such a manner that he could not retreat at all, and must wait my return from the next village, whither I went for ropes and a cart, to secure him properly, and to carry him off safe and alive, which perfectly succeeded.

You have heard, I dare say, of the hunters and sportsman's saint and protector, Saint Hubert; and of the noble stag, which appeared to him in the forest, with the holy cross between his antlers. I have paid my homages to that saint every year in good fellowship, and seen this stag a thousand times, either painted in churches or embroidered in the stars of his knights; so that upon honour and conscience of a good sportsman, I hardly know whether there may not have been formerly, or whether there are not such crossed stags even at this present day. But let me rather tell what I have seen myself. Having one day spent all my shot, I found myself unexpectedly in presence of a stately stag, looking at me so unconcernedly, as if he had known of my empty pouches. I charged immediately with

powder, and upon it a good handful of cherries, of which I had partly sucked the flesh as far as the hurry would permit. Thus I let fly at him, and hit him just on the middle of the forehead, between his antlers. It stunned him—he staggered— yet he made off. A year or two after I was with a party in the same forest—and behold a noble stag comes out with a fine full-grown cherry-tree between his antlers. I recollected my former adventure; looked upon him as my property; and brought him to the ground by one shot, which at once gave me the haunce and cherry-sauce; for the tree was covered with the richest fruit, the like I never had tasted before. Who knows but some passionate holy sportsman, or sporting abbot or bishop, may have shot, planted and fixed the cross between the antlers of Saint Hubert's stag in a manner similar to this? They always have been and still are famous for plantations of crosses and antlers; and, in a case of distress or dilemma, which too often happens to gallant sportsmen, one is apt to grasp at any thing for safety, and to try any expedient, rather than miss the favourable opportunity. I have many times found myself in that trying situation.

What do you say of this for example? Day-light and pow-der were spent one day in a Polish forest. When I was going home, a terrible bear made up to me in great speed, with open mouth, ready to fall upon me, all my pockets were searched in an instant for powder and ball, but in vain—I found nothing but two spare flints; one I flung with all my might into the monster's open jaws, down his throat. It gave him pain, and made him turn about, so that I could level the second at his back-door, which, indeed, I did with wonderful success, for it flew in, met the first flint in the stomach, struck fire, and blew up the bear with a terrible explosion. Though I came safe off that time, yet I should not wish to try it again, or venture against bears with no other defence.

There is a kind of fatality in it. The fiercest and most dan-gerous animals, generally come upon me when defenceless, as if they had a notion or foresight of it by way of instinct. Thus a frightful wolf rushed upon me so suddenly, and so close that I could do nothing but follow mechanical instinct, and thrust my fist into his open mouth. For safety's sake I pushed on and on, till my arm was fairly in, up to the shoulder. How should I disengage myself? I was not much pleased with my aukward situation—with a wolf face to face—our ogling was not of the most pleasant kind. If I withdrew my arm, then the animal would fly the more furiously upon me; that, I saw in his flaming eyes. In short, I laid hold of his intrails, turned him inside out like a glove and flung him to the ground, where I left him.

The same expedient would not have answered against a mad dog, which soon after came running against me in a narrow street at St Petersburgh. Run who can, I thought; and the better to run I threw off my fur cloak, and was safe within doors in an instant. I sent my servant for the cloak, and he put it in the wardrobe with my other cloaths. The day after I was amazed and frightened by Jacks bawling: 'For God's sake, Sir, your fur cloak is mad!' I hastened up to him, and found almost all my cloaths tossed about and torn to pieces. The fellow was perfectly right in his apprehensions about the fur cloak's madness. I saw him myself just then falling upon a fine full-dress suit, which he shook and tossed in an unmerciful manner.

All these narrow and lucky escapes, Gentlemen, were chances turned to advantage, by presence of mind and vigorous exertions; which taken together, as every body knows, makes the fortunate sportsman, sailor and soldier; but he would be a very blameable and imprudent sportsman, admiral or general, who would always depend upon chance and his stars, without troubling himself about those arts which are their particular pursuits, and without providing the very best implements, which insure success. I was not blameable either way; for I have always been as remarkable for the excellency of my horses, dogs, guns and swords, as for the proper manner of using and managing them, so that upon the whole I may hope to be remembered in the forest, upon the turf, and in the field. I shall not enter here into any detail of my stables, kennel, or armoury, but a favourite dog of mine I cannot help mentioning to you. It was a greyhound. I never had or saw a better one. He grew old in my service, and was not remarkable for his size, but the rather for his uncommon swiftness. I always coursed with him. Had you seen him, you must have admired him, and would not have wondered at my predilection, and at my coursing him so much. He run so fast, so much, and so long in my service, that he actually run off his legs, so that in the latter part of his life, I was under the necessity of working and using him only as a terrier, in which quality he still served me many years.

Whilst a greyhound—I must observe she was a bitch—She coursed one day a hare, which appeared to me uncommonly big. I pitied my poor bitch, she was big with pups, yet she would course as fast as ever. I could follow her on horseback only at a great distance. At once I heard a cry as it were of a pack of hounds—but so weak and faint, that I hardly knew what to make of it. Coming up at last, I was greatly surprised. The hare had littered in running; the same had happened to my bitch in coursing—and there were just as many leverets as pups. By instinct the former run, the latter coursed, and thus, I found myself in possession at once of six hares, and as many dogs, at the end of a course, which had only begun with one.

16

I remember this, my wonderful bitch, with the same pleasure and tenderness, as a superb Lithuanian horse, which no
money could have bought. He became mine by an accident,
which gave me an opportunity of shewing my horsemanship
to a great advantage. I was at Count Przobofsky's noble
country seat in Lithuania, and remained with the ladies at tea,
in the drawing room, while the gentlemen were down in the
yard, to see a young horse of blood, which was just arrived
from the stud. At once we heard a noise of distress—I hastened
down stairs, and found the horse so unruly that nobody durst
approach or mount him. The most resolute horsemen stood
dismayed and agast; despondency was expressed in every
countenance, when in one leap, I was on his back, frightened
him by surprize, and worked him quite into gentleness and
obedience, with the best display of horsemanship I was master
of. Fully to shew this to the ladies, and save them unnecessary
trouble, I forced him to leap in at one of the open windows of
the tea room, walked round several times, pace, trot, and
gallop; and at last made him mount the tea-table, there to
repeat his lessons, in a pretty style of miniature, which was exceedingly pleasing to the ladies, for he performed them amazingly well, and did not break either cup or saucer. It put me so
high in the opinion of the ladies, and so well in that of the
noble lord, that with his usual politeness he begged I would
accept of this young horse, and ride him full career to conquest and honor, in the campaign against the Turks, which
was soon to be opened, under the command of Count
Munich.

I could not indeed have received a more agreeable present,

nor a more ominous one at the opening of that campaign, in which I made my apprenticeship as a soldier. A horse so gentle, so spirited, and so fierce—at once a lamb and a Bucephalus, put me always in mind of the soldier's and the gentleman's duty, of young Alexander and of the astonishing things he performed in the field.

We took the field, among several other reasons it seems, with an intention to retrieve the character of the Russian arms, which had been blemished a little by Czar Peter's last campaign on the Pruth—and this we fully accomplished by several very fatiguing and glorious campaigns under the command of that great general I mentioned before.

Modesty forbids individuals, to arrogate to themselves great successes or victories, the glory of which is generally engrossed by the commander, nay, which is rather aukward, by kings and queens, who never smelt gun-powder, but at the field days and reviews of their troops, never saw a field of battle or an enemy in battle array.

Nor do I claim any particular share of glory in the great engagements with the enemy. We all did our duty, which, in the patriots, soldiers, and gentleman's language, is a very comprehensive word of great honour, meaning and import, and of which the generality of idle quidnuncs and coffee-house politicians, can hardly form any but a very mean and contemptible idea. However, having had the command of a

body of huzars, I have been on several expeditions, with dis-
cretionary powers; and the success I then met with, is, I think,
fairly, and only to be put to my account, and to that of the
brave fellows whom I led to conquest and to victory. We had
very hot work once in the van of the army, when we drove
the Turks into Oczakow. My spirited Lithuanian had almost
brought me into a scrape. I had an advanced forepost, and saw
the enemy coming against me in a cloud of dust, which left
me rather uncertain about their actual numbers and real intentions. To wrap myself up in a similar cloud of dust was
common prudence, but would not have much advanced my
knowledge, or answered the end for which I had been sent
out. Therefore I let my flankers on both wings spread to the
right and left, and make what dust they could, and I myself
led on straight upon the enemy, to have a nearer sight of them;
and that I had, gentlemen! for they stood and fought, till for
fear of my flankers, they began to move off rather disorderly.
This was the moment to fall upon them with spirit—We
broke them entirely, made a terrible havock amongst them—
and drove them not only back to a walled town in their rear,
but even through it, contrary to our most sanguine expectation.

By reason of the swiftness of my Lithuanian I had been
foremost in the pursuit; and seeing the enemy fairly flying
through the opposite gate, I thought it would be prudent to
stop in the market-place to order the trumpet to rendezvous.
I stopt, gentlemen, but judge of my astonishment, when in
this market-place I saw neither trumpet nor any living body
of my huzars about me. Are they scouring the other streets? or

what is become of them? they could not be far off, and must, at all events, soon join me. In that expectation I walked my panting Lithuanian to a spring in the market-place, and let him drink. He drunk uncommonly—with an eagerness not to be satisfied, but natural enough, for when I looked round for my men, what should I see, gentlemen? the hind part of the poor creature, croup and legs were missing, as if he had been cut in two, and the water run out as it came in, without either refreshing him or doing him any good. How it could have happened was quite a mystery to me, till I returned with him to the town gate. There I saw that when I rushed in peace meal with the flying enemy, they had dropt the port-cullis, and unperceived by me, and the spirited animal, it had totally cut off his hind part, which lay still quivering on the outside of the gate. It would have been an irreparable loss, had not our farrier contrived to bring both parts together while hot. He sowed them up with sprigs and young shoots of laurels that were just at hand—the wound healed and what could not have happened, but to so glorious a horse, the sprigs took root in his body, grew up, and formed a bower over me, so that afterwards I could go upon many other expeditions in the shade of my own and my horse's laurels.

But gentlemen, for all that; I was not always successful. I had even the misfortune to be overpowered by numbers, to be made prisoner of war; and what is worse, but always usual among the Turks, to be sold for a slave. In that state of humiliation, my daily task was not very hard, and laborious, but rather singular and irksome. It was to drive the Sultan's bees every morning to their pasture grounds, to attend them all the day long and against night to drive them back to their hives. One evening I missed a bee, and soon observed that two bears had fallen upon her, to tear her to pieces for the honey she carried. I had nothing like an offensive weapon in my hands, but the silver hatchet, which is the badge of the Sultan's gardeners and farmers. I threw it at the robbers with an intention to frighten them away, and set the poor bee at liberty; but by an unlucky turn of my arm, it flew upward—and flew, and flew, till it reached the moon. How should I recover it? How fetch it down again? I recollected that Turkey beans grew very quick, and run up to an astonishing height. I planted one immediately, it grew and actually fastened itself to one of the moon's horns. I had no more to do now, but to climb up by it into the moon, where I safely arrived. I had a troublesome piece of work of it, before I could find my silver hatchet in a place where every thing has the brightness of silver. At last however I found it in a heap of chaf and chopped straw. I was now for returning, but alas, the heat of the sun had dried up my bean; it was totally useless for my descent; so I fell to work, and twisted me a rope of that chopped straw, as long and well as I could make it. This I fastened to one of the moon's horns, and slid down to the end of it. Here I held myself fast with the left hand, and with the hatchet in my right, I cut the long, now useless end of the upper part, which when tied to the lower end brought me a good deal lower. However, this repeated splicing and tying of the rope did not improve its quality nor bring me down to the Sultan's farms. I was still a couple of miles in the clouds when it broke, and with such violence I fell to the ground that I found myself stunned, and in a hole nine fathoms under grass, when I recovered, hardly knowing how to get out again. There was no other way than to go home for a spade and to dig me out by slopes, which I fortunately accomplished, before I had been so much as missed by the steward.

Peace was soon after concluded with the Turks, and it was favourable to Russia in spite of French politics. I recovered my liberty and left St Petersburgh at the time of that singular revolution about forty years since, when the emperor in his cradle, his mother, the duke of Brunswick her father, field marshal Munich, and many others were sent to Siberia. The winter was then so uncommonly severe all over Europe, that ever since the sun seems to be frost-bitten—At my return to this place, I felt on the road greater inconveniences than those

I had experienced in my setting out for Russia. One effect of the frost which I then observed, is rather an object for philosophical speculation. I travelled post day and night, and finding myself engaged in a narrow lane, I bid the postilion give a signal with his horn, that other travellers might not meet or stop us in the narrow passage. He blew with all his might, but all his endeavours were in vain. He could not make the horn speak, which, as he pretended to be a good performer, was as unaccountable to him, as to me, and rather unfortunately, for soon after we found ourselves in the presence of another coach coming the other way. It was very troublesome for both parties in this horrid weather, for there was no proceeding either way, without taking the carriages to pieces and putting them together again, past each other. My poor postilion and every body was almost froze to death. However we reached the much-looked-for stage, without further accident, and well pleased and happy in our minds, we all of us hastened to warm and refresh ourselves.

The postilion hung his great coat and horn on a peg and sate down near the kitchen fire, to forget and drown his cares. I sat down on the other side doing the same. Suddenly we heard a *Tereng! tereng, teng, teng!* We looked round, and now found the reason, why the postilion had not been able to sound his horn. His tunes were frozen up in the horn, and came out now by thawing, plain enough, and much to the credit of the driver, so that the honest fellow entertained us for some time with a variety of tunes, without putting his mouth to the horn. The King of Prussia's march—Over the hill and over the dale—An evening hymn, and many other favourite tunes came out, and the thawing entertainment concluded, as I shall this short account of my Russian travels with

God bless Great George our King.

II

SEA ADVENTURES

Some travellers are apt to advance more than is perhaps strictly true, and if any of the company entertain a doubt of my veracity, I shall only say to such unbelievers, I pity their want of faith, and must request, if there be any such present, that they will take their leave before I begin my NAVAL ADVENTURES all of which are equally authentic

I embarked at Portsmouth in a first-rate English man-of-war, of one hundred guns, and fourteen hundred men, for North America. Nothing worth relating happened till we arrived within three hundred leagues of the river St Laurence, when the ship struck with amazing force against (as we supposed) a rock; however, upon heaving the lead we could find no bottom, even with three hundred fathom. What made this circumstance the more wonderful, and indeed beyond all comprehension, was, that the violence of the shock was such that we lost our rudder, broke our bow sprit in the middle, and split all our masts from top to bottom, two of which went by the board: a poor fellow, who was aloft furling the mainsheet, was flung at least three leagues from the ship; but he fortunately saved his life by laying hold of the tail of a large sea-gull, who brought him back, and lodged him on the very spot from whence he was thrown. Another proof of the violence of the shock was the force with which the people between decks were driven against the floors above them: my head particularly was pressed into my stomach, where it continued some months before it recovered its natural situation. Whilst we were all in a state of astonishment at the general and unaccountable confusion in which we were involved, the whole was suddenly explained by the appearance of a large whale, who had been basking, asleep, within sixteen feet of the surface of the water. This animal was so much displeased with the disturbance which our ship had given him (for in our passage we had with our rudder scratched his nose) that he beat in all the gallery and part of the quarter-deck with his tail, and almost at the same instant took the main-sheet anchor, which was suspended, as it usually is, from the head, between his teeth, and ran away with the ship, at least sixty leagues, at the rate of twelve leagues an hour, when fortunately the cable broke, and we lost both the whale and the anchor. However, upon our return to Europe, some months after, we found the same whale, within a few leagues of the same spot, floating dead upon the water; it measured above half a mile in length. As we could take but a small quantity of such a monstrous animal on board, we got our boats out, and with much difficulty cut off his head, where, to our great joy, we found the anchor, and above forty fathom of the cable, concealed on the left side of his mouth, just under his tongue. (Perhaps this was the cause of his death, as that side of his tongue was much swelled, with a great degree of inflammation.) This was the only extraordinary circumstance that happened on this voyage. One part of our distress however I had like to have

25

forgot: while the whale was running away with the ship, she sprung a leak, and the water poured in so fast, that all our pumps could not keep us from sinking; it was however my good fortune to discover it first. I found it a large hole about a foot diameter; you will naturally suppose this circumstance gives me infinite pleasure, when I inform you, that this noble vessel was preserved, with all its crew, by a most fortunate thought! In short, I completely filled it with my ——, without taking off my small-clothes, and could have dispensed with it had it been larger; nor will you be surprised when I inform you I am descended from Dutch parents.

My situation, while I sat there, was rather cool, but the carpenter's art soon relieved me.

I was once in great danger of being lost in a most singular manner in the Mediterranean: I was bathing in that pleasant sea near Marseilles one summer's afternoon, when I discovered a very large fish, with his jaws quite extended, approaching me with the greatest velocity; there was no time to be lost, nor could I possibly avoid him. I immediately reduced myself to as small a size as possible, by closing my feet and placing my hands also near my sides, in which position I passed directly between his jaws, and into his stomach, where I remained some time in total darkness, and comfortably warm, as you may imagine; at last it occurred to me, that by giving him pain he would be glad to get rid of me: as I had plenty of room, I played my pranks, such as tumbling, hop, step, and jump, &c., but nothing seemed to disturb him so much as the quick motion of my feet in attempting to dance a hornpipe; soon after I began he put me out, by sudden fits and starts:

I persevered; at last he roared horridly, and stood up almost perpendicular in the water, with his head and shoulders exposed, by which he was discovered by the people on board an Italian trader, then sailing by, who harpooned him in a few minutes. As soon as he was brought on board, I heard the crew consulting how they should cut him up, so as to preserve the greatest quantity of oil. As I understood Italian, I was in most dreadful apprehensions lest their weapons employed in this business should destroy me also; therefore I stood as near the centre as possible, for there was room enough for a dozen men in this creature's stomach, and I naturally imagined they would begin with the extremities: however, my fears were soon dispersed, for they began by opening the bottom of the belly. As soon as I perceived a glimmering of light I called out lustily to be released from a situation in which I was now almost suffocated. It is impossible for me to do justice to the degree and kind of astonishment which sat upon every countenance at hearing a human voice issue from a fish, but more so at seeing a naked man walk upright out of his body: in short, gentlemen, I told them the whole story, as I have done you, whilst amazement struck them dumb.

After taking some refreshment, and jumping into the sea to cleanse myself, I swam to my clothes, which lay where I had left them on the shore. As near as I can calculate, I was near four hours and a half confined in the stomach of this animal.

When I was in the service of the Turks I frequently amused myself in a pleasure-barge on the Marmora, which commands a view of the whole city of Constantinople, including the

Grand Seignior's Seraglio. One morning, as I was admiring the beauty and serenity of the sky, I observed a globular substance in the air, which appeared to be about the size of a twelve-inch globe, with something suspended from it. I immediately took up my largest and longest barrel fowling piece, which I never travel or make even an excursion without, if I can help it: I charged it with ball, and fired at the globe; but to no purpose, the object being at too great a distance. I then put in a double quantity of powder, and five or six balls: this second attempt succeeded; all the balls took effect, and tore one side open, and brought it down. Judge my surprise, when a most elegant gilt car, with a man in it, and part of a sheep which seemed to have been roasted, fell within two yards of me: when my astonishment had in some degree subsided, I ordered my people to row close to this strange aerial traveller.

I took him on board my barge (he was a native of France): he was much indisposed from his sudden fall into the sea, and incapable of speaking; after some time, however, he recovered and gave the following account of himself, viz: 'About seven or eight days since, I cannot tell which, for I have lost my reckoning, having been most of the time where the sun never sets, I ascended from the Land's-End in Cornwall, in the island of GREAT BRITAIN, in the car from which I have been just taken, suspended from a very large balloon, and took a sheep with me, to try atmospheric experiments upon: unfortunately, the wind changed within ten minutes after my ascent; and, instead of driving towards Exeter, where I intended to land, I was driven towards the sea, over which I suppose I have continued ever since, but much too high to make observations.

'The calls of hunger were so pressing, that the intended experiments upon heat and respiration gave way to them. I was obliged, on the third day, to kill the sheep for food; and being at that time infinitely above the moon, and for upwards of sixteen hours after so very near the sun that it scorched my eyebrows, I placed the carcass, taking care to skin it first, in that part of the car where the sun had sufficient power, or, in other words, where the balloon did not shade it from the sun, by which method it was well roasted in about two hours. This has been my food ever since.' Here he paused, and seemed lost in viewing the objects about him. When I told him the buildings before us were the Grand Seignior's Seraglio at Constantinople, he seemed exceedingly affected, as he had supposed himself in a very different situation. 'The cause,' added he, 'of my long flight, was owing to the failure of a string which was fixed to a valve in the balloon, intended to let out the inflammable air; and if it had not been fired at, and rent in the manner before mentioned, I might, like Mahomet, have been suspended between heaven and earth till doomsday.'

The Grand Seignior, to whom I was introduced by the Imperial, Russian, and French ambassadors, employed me to negotiate a matter of great importance at Grand Cairo, and which was of such a nature that it must ever remain a secret.

I went there in great state by land; where having completed the business, I dismissed almost all my attendants, and returned like a private gentleman: the weather was delightful, and that famous river the Nile was beautiful beyond all description; in short, I was tempted to hire a barge to descend by water to Alexandria. On the third day of my voyage the river began to rise most amazingly (you have all heard, I presume, of the annual overflowing of the Nile), and on the next day it spread the whole country for many leagues on each side! On the fifth, at sunrise, my barge became entangled with what I at first took for shrubs; but as the light became stronger I found myself surrounded by almonds, which were perfectly ripe, and in the highest perfection. Upon plumbing with a line my people found we were at least sixty feet from the ground, and unable to advance or retreat. At about eight or nine o'clock, as near as I could judge by the altitude of the sun, the wind rose suddenly, and canted our barge on one side: here she filled, and I saw no more of her for some time. Fortunately we all saved ourselves (six men and two boys) by clinging to the tree, the boughs of which were equal to our weight, though not to that of the barge: in this situation we continued six weeks and three days, living upon the almonds; I need not inform you we had plenty of water. On the forty-second day of our distress the water fell as rapidly as it had risen, and on the forty-sixth we were able to venture down upon terra firma. Our barge was the first pleasing object we saw, about two hundred yards from the spot where she sunk. After drying everything that was useful by the heat of the sun, and loading ourselves with necessaries from the stores on board, we set out to recover our lost ground; and found, by the nearest calculation, we had been carried over garden-walls, and a variety of enclosures, above one hundred and fifty miles. In four days, after a very tiresome journey on foot, with thin shoes, we reached the river, which was now confined to its banks, related our adventures to a Bey, who kindly accommodated all our wants, and sent us forward in a barge of his own. In six days more we arrived at Alexandria, where we took shipping for Constantinople. I was received kindly by

the grand Seignior, and had the honour of seeing the seraglio, to which his highness introduced me himself, and presented me with as many ladies, his wives not excepted, as I thought proper to select for my own amusement and that of my friends also.

As soon as the Baron had related the latest story he retired, and left the company much diverted and in good spirits. After each man had expressed himself as he thought proper upon the extraordinary entertainment he had given them, one of the company, a near relation, who attended him on his last journey to Turkey, observed that near Constantinople they have an amazing piece of ordnance, of which Baron de Tott, in his memoirs, recently published, takes particular notice.

'What he says of it, as near as my memory will serve me, is this: "The Turks had placed below the castle, and near the city, on the banks of *Simois*, a celebrated river, an enormous piece of ordnance, cast in brass, which would carry a marble ball of *eleven hundred pounds weight*. I was inclined," says Tott, "to fire it, but I was willing first to judge of its effect; the crowd about me trembled at this proposal, as they asserted it would overthrow not only the castle, but the city also: at length their fears in part subsided, and I was permitted to discharge it. It required not less than *three hundred and thirty pounds weight of powder*, and the ball weighed, as before mentioned, *eleven hundredweight*. When the engineer brought the priming, the crowds who were about me retreated back as fast as they could; nay, it was with the utmost difficulty I persuaded the Pacha, who came on purpose, there was no danger: even the engineer, who was to discharge it by my

32

direction, was considerably alarmed. I took my stand on some stone-work behind the cannon, gave the signal, and felt a shock like that of an *earthquake*! At the distance of three hundred fathom, the ball burst into three pieces; the fragments crossed the Strait, rebounded on the opposite mountain, and left the surface of the water all in a foam through the whole breadth of the channel."

'This, gentlemen, is, as near as I can recollect, Baron Tott's account of the largest cannon in the known world. Now, when I was there not long since, the anecdote of Tott's firing this tremendous piece was mentioned as a proof of that gentleman's extraordinary courage.

'My friend Munchausen, who was determined not to be out-done by a Frenchman, therefore took this very piece upon his shoulder, and, after balancing it properly, jumped into the sea with it, and swam to the opposite shore, from whence he unfortunately attempted to throw it back into its former place: I say unfortunately, for it slipped a little in his hand just as he was going to discharge it, and in consequence of that it fell into the middle of the channel, where it now lies, without a prospect of ever recovering it; and notwithstanding the high favour he was in with the Grand Seignior, as before mentioned, this cruel Turk, as soon as he heard of the loss of his famous piece of ordnance, issued an order to cut off his head. He was immediately informed of it by one of the Sultanas, with whom he was become a great favourite, and she secreted us in her apartment while the officer charged with his execution was, with his assistants, in search of him.

'That very night we both made our escape on board a vessel bound to Venice, which was then weighing anchor to proceed on her voyage.'

'This story, gentlemen, the Baron is not fond of mentioning, as he miscarried in his attempt and was very near losing his life into the bargain; however, as it contains no impeachment of his honour, I frequently relate it in his absence.

'Now, gentlemen, you all know the Baron, and can have no doubt of his veracity; lest any of you should entertain any scruples about mine, a circumstance which I can scarcely suppose, I will let you know who I am. I have already informed you that I am related to the Baron.

'My reputed father[1] was a native of Berne, in Switzerland; his profession was that of a surveyor of the streets, lanes, and alleys, vulgarly called a *scavenger*. My mother was a native of the mountains of Savoy, and had a most beautiful large wen on her neck, common to both sexes in that part of the world; she left her parents when young, and sought her fortune in the same city which gave my father birth: she maintained herself while single by acts of kindness to our sex, for she never was known to refuse them any favour they asked, provided they did but pay her some compliment before hand. This lovely couple met by accident in the street, in consequence of their being both intoxicated, for by reeling to one centre, they threw each other down; this created mutual abuse, in which they were complete adepts; they were both carried to the watch-house, and afterwards to the house of correction; they soon saw the folly of quarrelling, made it up, became fond of each other, and married; but madam returning to her old tricks, my father, who had high notions of honour, soon separated himself from her; she then joined a family who strolled about with a puppet-show. In time she arrived at

[1] Editions vary in their choice of victim for this story. Sometimes it is de Tott, sometimes the Baron himself, sometimes, as in the Third Edition which is followed here, the Baron's Friend.

Rome, where she kept an oyster-stand. You have all heard, no doubt, of Pope Ganganelli, commonly called Clement XIV[1]: he was remarkably fond of oysters. One Good Friday, as he was passing through this famous city in state, to assist at high mass at St Peter's church, he saw this woman's oysters (which were remarkably fine and fresh); he could not proceed without tasting them; there were about five thousand people in his train; he ordered them all to stop, and sent word to the church he could not attend mass till next day; then alighting from his horse (for the Pope always rides on horseback upon these occasions) he went into her stall, and ate every oyster she had there, and afterwards retired into the cellar where she had a few more. This subterraneous apartment was her kitchen, parlour, and bed-chamber. He liked his situation so much that he discharged all his attendants, and to make short of the story, His Holiness passed the whole night with her! Before they parted he gave her absolution, not only for every sin she had, but all she might hereafter commit.

'Now, gentlemen, I have my mother's word for it (and her honour cannot be doubted), that I am the fruit of that amour.'

III

FURTHER SURPRISING ADVENTURES

During the late siege of Gibraltar I went with a provision-fleet, under Lord Rodney's command, to see my old friend General Elliot, who has, by his distinguished defence of that place, acquired laurels that can never fade. After the usual

[1] Antonio Ganganelli, Pope Clement XIV, reigned 1769–1774. He was for many years the target of anonymous abuse, and fictitious letters published under his name in 1776 gained him a posthumous notoriety.

joy which generally attends the meeting of old friends had subsided, I went to examine the state of the garrison, and view the operations of the enemy, for which purpose the General accompanied me. I had brought a most excellent refracting telescope with me from London, purchased of Dollond,[1] by the help of which I found the enemy were going to discharge a thirty-six pounder at the spot where we stood. I told the General what they were about; he looked through the glass also, and found my conjectures right. I immediately, by his permission, ordered a forty-eight pounder to be brought from a neighbouring battery, which I placed with so much exactness (having long studied the art of gunnery) that I was sure of my mark.

I continued watching the enemy till I saw the match placed at the touch-hole of their piece; at that very instant I gave the signal for our gun to be fired also. About midway between the two pieces of cannon the balls struck each other with amazing force, and the effect was astonishing! The enemy's ball recoiled back with such violence as to kill the man who had discharged it, by carrying his head fairly off, with sixteen others which it met with in its progress to the Barbary Coast; where its force, after passing through three masts of vessels that then lay in a line behind each other in the harbour, was so much spent, that it only broke its way through the roof of a poor labourer's hut, about two hundred yards inland, and destroyed a few teeth an old woman had left, who lay asleep upon her back with her mouth open. The ball lodged in her throat. Her husband soon after came home, and endeavoured to extract it; but finding that impracticable, by the assistance of a rammer he forced it into her stomach from whence it was discharged downwards in a

[1] This famous firm had at this time just established its reputation.

natural way. Our ball did excellent service; for it not only repelled the other in the manner just described; but proceeding as I intended it should, it dismounted the very piece of cannon that had been just employed against us, and forced it into the hold of the ship, where it fell with so much force as to break its way through the bottom. The ship immediately filled and sunk, with above a thousand Spanish sailors on board, besides a considerable number of soldiers. This, to be sure, was a most extraordinary exploit: I will not, however, take the whole merit to myself; my judgment was the principal engine, but chance assisted me a little; for I afterwards found, that the man who charged our forty-eight pounder put in, by mistake, a double quantity of powder, else we could never have succeeded so much beyond all expectation, especially in repelling the enemy's ball.

General Elliot would have given me a commission for this singular piece of service; but I declined everything, except his thanks, which I received at a crowded table of officers at supper on the evening of that very day.

As I am very partial to the English, who are beyond all doubt a brave people, I determined not to take my leave of the garrison till I had rendered them another piece of service, and in about three weeks an opportunity presented itself. I dressed myself in the habit of a *Popish Priest*, and at about one o'clock in the morning stole out of the garrison, passed the enemy's lines, and arrived in the middle of their camp, where I entered the tent in which the Prince d'Artois[1] was, with the commander-in-chief, and several other officers, in deep coun-

[1] Properly the Count d'Artois and later Charles X of France. He was at that time with the army besieging Gibraltar.

cil, concerning a plan to storm the garrison next morning. My disguise was my protection; they suffered me to continue there, hearing everything that passed, till they went to their several beds. When I found the whole camp, and even the sentinels, were wrapped up in the arms of Morpheus, I began my work, which was that of dismounting all their cannon (above three hundred pieces) from forty-eight to twenty-four pounders, and throwing them three leagues into the sea. Having no assistance, I found this the hardest task I ever undertook. I then piled all the carriages together in the centre of the camp, which, to prevent the noise of the wheels being heard, I carried in pairs under my arms: and a noble appearance they made, as high at least as the rock of Gibraltar. I then lighted a match by striking a flint stone, situated twenty feet from the ground (in an old wall built by the Moors when they invaded Spain), with the breech of an iron eight-and-forty pounder, and so set fire to the whole pile. I forgot to inform you that I threw all their ammunition-wagons upon the top.

Before I applied the lighted match I had laid the combustibles at the bottom so judiciously, that the whole was in a blaze in a moment. To prevent suspicion, I was one of the first to express my surprise. The whole camp was, as you may imagine, petrified with astonishment; the general conclusion was, that their sentinels had been bribed, and that seven or eight regiments of the garrison had been employed in this horrid destruction of their artillery. Mr Drinkwater, in his account of this famous siege, mentions the enemy sustaining a great loss by a fire which happened in their camp, but never knew the cause[1]; how should he? as I never divulged it before

[1] The incident mentioned is described by Drinkwater as having occurred on August 19th, 1782. 'A small magazine blew up in the enemy's camp, near Buena Vista, which set a hut on fire.'

(though I alone saved Gibraltar by this night's business), not even to General Elliot. The Count d'Artois and all his attendants ran away in their fright, and never stopped on the road till they reached Paris, which they did in about a fortnight: this dreadful conflagration had such an effect upon them that they were incapable of taking the least refreshment for three months after, but, chameleon-like, lived upon the air.

If any gentleman will say he doubts the truth of this story, I will fine him a gallon of brandy and make him drink it at one draught.

About two months after I had done the besieged this service, one morning, as I sat at breakfast with General Elliot, a shell (for I had not time to destroy their mortars as well as their cannon) entered the apartment we were sitting in; it lodged upon our table. The General, as most men would do, quitted the room directly; but I took it up before it burst, and carried it to the top of the rock; when, looking over the enemy's camp, on an eminence near the sea-coast, I observed a considerable number of people, but could not, with my naked eye, discover how they were employed. I had recourse again to my telescope, when I found that two of our officers, one a general, the other a colonel, with whom I had spent the preceding evening, and who went out into the enemy's camp about midnight as spies, were taken, and then were actually going to be executed on a gibbet. I found the distance too great to throw the shell with my hand, but most fortunately recollecting that I had the very sling in my pocket which assisted David in slaying Goliath, I placed the shell in it, and immediately threw it in the midst of them: it burst as it fell, and destroyed all present, except the two culprits, who were saved by being suspended so high, for they were just turned off: however, one of the pieces of the shell fled with such force against the foot of the gibbet, that it immediately brought it down. Our two friends no sooner felt terra firma, than they looked about for the cause; and finding their guards, executioner, and all, had taken it in their heads to die first, they directly extricated each other from their disgraceful cords, and then ran down to the sea-shore, seized a Spanish boat with two men in it, and made them row to one of our ships, which they did with great safety; and in a few minutes after, when I was relating to General Elliot how I had acted, they both took us by the hand, and, after mutual congratulations, we retired to spend the day with festivity. As to the SLING, I have bequeathed it as a relick of inestimable value, to be hung up in LIBERTY HALL, and hereafter used, as often as necessary, in the destruction of all TYRANTS and those who are base enough to act under them.

You wish (I can see by your countenances) I would inform you how I became possessed of such a treasure as the sling just mentioned. Here facts must be held sacred. Thus then it was: I am a descendant of the wife of Uriah, whom we all know David was intimate with; she had several children by his majesty; they quarrelled once upon a matter of the first consequence, viz., the spot where Noah's ark was built, and where it rested after the flood. A separation consequently ensued. She had often heard him speak of this sling as his most valuable treasure: this she stole the night they parted; it was missed before she got out of his dominions, and she was pursued by no less than six of the king's body-guards: however, by using it herself she hit the first of them (for one was more active in the pursuit than the rest) where David did Goliath, and killed him on the spot. His companions were so alarmed at his fall that they retired, and left Uriah's wife to pursue her journey. She took with her, I should have informed you before, her favourite son by his connexion, to whom she bequeathed the sling; and thus it has, without interruption, descended from father to son till it came into my possession. One of its possessors, my great great great grandfather, who lived about two hundred and fifty years ago, was upon a visit to England, and became intimate with a poet, who was a great deer-stealer; I think his name was Shakespeare: he frequently borrowed this sling, and with it killed so much of Sir Thomas Lucy's venison, that he narrowly escaped the fate of my two friends at Gibraltar. Poor Shakespeare was imprisoned, and my ancestor obtained his freedom in a very singular manner. Queen Elizabeth was then on the throne, but grown so indolent, that every trifling matter was become a trouble to her; dressing, undressing, eating, drinking, and some other offices which shall be nameless, made life a burden to her; all these things he enabled her to do without, or by a deputy! and what do you think was the only return she could prevail upon him to accept for such eminent services? setting Shakespeare at liberty! Such was his affection for that famous writer, that he would have shortened his own days to add to the number of his friend's.

I do not hear that any of the queen's subjects, particularly the *beef-eaters*, as they are vulgarly called to this day, however they might be struck with the novelty at the time, much approved of her living totally without food. She did not survive the practice herself above seven years and a half.

My father, who was the immediate possessor of this sling before me, told me the following anecdote:

He was walking by the sea-shore at Harwich, with this sling in his pocket; before his paces had covered a mile he was attacked by a fierce animal called a seahorse, open-mouthed, who ran at him with great fury; he hesitated a moment, then took out his sling, retreated back about a hundred yards, stooped for a couple of pebbles, of which there were plenty under his feet, and slung them both so dexterously at the animal, that each stone put out an eye, and lodged in the cavities which their removal had occasioned. He now got upon its back, and drove him into the sea; for the moment he lost his sight he lost also his ferocity, and became as tame as possible: the sling was placed as a bridle in his mouth; he was guided with the greatest facility across the ocean, and in less than three hours they both arrived on the opposite shore, which is about thirty leagues. The master of the *Three Cups*, at Helvoetsluys, in Holland, purchased this marine horse, to make an exhibition of, for seven hundred ducats, which was upwards of three hundred pounds, and the next day my father paid his passage back in the packet to Harwich.

My father made several curious observations in this passage, which I will relate hereafter.

This famous sling makes the possessor equal to any task he is desirous of performing.

I made a balloon of such extensive dimensions, that an account of the silk it contained would exceed all credibility; every mercer's shop and weaver's stock in London, West-

42

minster, and Spitalfields contributed to it: with this balloon and my sling I played many tricks, such as taking one house from its station, and placing another in its stead, without disturbing the inhabitants, who were generally asleep, or too much employed to observe the peregrinations of their habitations. When the sentinel at Windsor Castle heard St Paul's clock strike thirteen, it was through my dexterity; I brought the buildings nearly together that night, by placing the castle in St George's Fields, and carried it back again before daylight, without waking any of the inhabitants; notwithstanding these exploits, I should have kept my balloon and its properties a secret, if Montgolfier had not made the art of flying so public.

On the 30th of September, when the College of Physicians chose their annual officers, and dined sumptuously together, I filled my balloon, brought it over the dome of their building, clapped the sling round the golden ball at the top, fastening the other end of it to the balloon and immediately ascended with the whole college to an immense height, where I kept them upwards of three months. You will naturally inquire what they did for food such a length of time? To this I answer, Had I kept them suspended twice the time, they would have experienced no inconvenience on that account, so amply, or rather extravagantly, had they spread their table for that day's feasting.

Though this was meant as an innocent frolic, it was productive of much mischief to several respectable characters amongst the clergy, undertakers, sextons, and grave-diggers: they were, it must be acknowledged, sufferers; for it is a well-known fact, that during the three months the college was suspended in the air, and therefore incapable of attending their patients, no deaths happened, except a few who fell before the scythe of

Father Time, and some melancholy objects who, perhaps to avoid some trifling inconvenience here, laid the hands of violence upon themselves, and plunged into misery infinitely greater than that which they hoped by such a rash step to avoid, without a moment's consideration.

If the apothecaries had not been very active during the above time, half the undertakers in all probability would have been bankrupts.

On my return from Gibraltar I travelled by way of France to England. Being a foreigner, this was not attended with any inconvenience to me.[1] I found, in the harbour of Calais, a ship

[1] The Baron must be imagined as travelling during the War of American Independence which ended in 1783.

45

just arrived with a number of English sailors as prisoners of war. I immediately conceived an idea of giving these brave fellows their liberty, which I accomplished as follows: After forming a pair of large wings, each of them forty yards long, and fourteen wide, and annexing them to myself, I mounted at break of day, when every creature, even the watch upon deck, was fast asleep. As I hovered over the ship I fastened three grappling irons to the tops of the three masts with my sling, and fairly lifted her several yards out of the water, and then proceeded across to Dover, where I arrived in half an hour! Having no further occasion for these wings, I made them a present to the Governor of Dover Castle, where they are now exhibited to the curious.

As to the prisoners, and the Frenchmen who guarded them, they did not awake till they had been near two hours on Dover Pier. The moment the English understood their situation they changed places with their guard, and took back what they had been plundered of, *but no more,* for they were too generous to retaliate and plunder them in return.

We all remember Captain Phipps's (now Lord Mulgrave) last voyage of discovery to the north. I accompanied the captain, not as an officer, but a private friend. When we arrived in a high northern latitude I was viewing the objects around me with the telescope which I introduced to your notice in my Gibraltar adventures. I thought I saw two large white bears in violent action upon a body of ice considerably above the masts, and about half a league distance. I immediately took my carbine, slung it across my shoulder, and ascended the ice. When I arrived at the top, the unevenness of the surface made my approach to those animals troublesome and hazardous beyond expression: sometimes hideous cavities opposed me, which I was obliged to spring over; in other parts the surface was as smooth as a mirror, and I was continually falling: as I approached near enough to reach them, I found they were only at play. I immediately began to calculate the value of their skins, for they were each as large as a well-fed ox: unfortunately, at the very instant I was presenting my carbine my right foot slipped, I fell upon my back, and the violence of the blow deprived me totally of my senses for nearly half an hour; however, when I recovered, judge of my surprise at finding one of those large animals I have been just describing had turned me upon my face, and was just laying hold of the waistband of my breeches, which were then new and made of leather: he was certainly going to carry me feet foremost, God knows where, when I took this knife (showing a large clasp knife) out of my side pocket, made a chop at one of his hind-feet, and cut off three of his toes; he immediately let me drop and roared most horridly. I took up my carbine and fired at him as he ran off; he fell directly. The noise of the piece roused several thousands of these white bears, who were asleep upon the ice within half a mile of me; they came immediately to the spot. There was no time to be lost. A most fortunate thought arrived in my pericranium just at that instant. I took off the skin and head of the dead bear in half the time that some people would be in skinning a rabbit, and wrapped myself in it, placing my own head directly under Bruin's; the whole herd came round me immediately, and my apprehensions threw me into a most piteous situation to be sure: however, my scheme turned out a most admirable one for my own safety. They all came smelling, and evidently took me for a brother Bruin; I wanted nothing but bulk to make an excellent counterfeit: however, I saw several cubs amongst them not much larger than myself. After they had all smelt me, and the body of their deceased companion, whose skin was now become my protector, we seemed very sociable, and I found I could mimic all their actions tolerably well; but at growling, roaring, and hugging they were quite my masters. I began now to think how I might turn the general confidence which I had created amongst these animals to my advantage.

I had heard an old army surgeon say a wound in the spine was instant death. I now determined to try the experiment, and had again recourse to my knife, with which I struck the largest in the back of the neck, near the shoulders, but under great apprehensions, not doubting but the creature would, if he survived the stab, tear me to pieces. However, I was remarkably fortunate, for he fell dead at my feet without making the least noise. I was now resolved to demolish them every one in the same manner, which I accomplished without the least difficulty; for although they saw their companions fall, they had no suspicion of either the cause or the effect. When they all lay dead before me, I felt myself a second Sampson, having slain my thousands.

To make short of the story, I went back to the ship, and borrowed three parts of the crew to assist me in skinning them, and carrying the hams on board, which we did in a few hours, and loaded the ship with them. As to the other parts of the animals, they were thrown into the sea, though I doubt not but the whole would eat as well as the legs, were they properly cured.

As soon as we returned I sent some of the hams, in the captain's name, to the Lords of the Admiralty, others to the Lords of the Treasury, some to the Lord Mayor and Corporation of London, a few to each of the trading companies, and the remainder to my particular friends, from all of whom I received warm thanks; but from the city I was honoured with substantial notice, viz., an invitation to dine at Guildhall annually on Lord Mayor's day.

The bear-skins I sent to the Empress of Russia[1], to clothe her majesty and her court in the winter, for which she wrote me a letter of thanks with her own hand, and sent it by an ambassador extraordinary, inviting me to share the honours of her bed and crown; but as I never was ambitious of royal dignity, I declined her majesty's favour in the politest terms. The same ambassador had orders to wait and bring my answer to her majesty *personally*, upon which business he was absent about three months: her majesty's reply convinced me of the strength of her affections, and the dignity of her mind; her late indisposition was entirely owing (as she, kind creature! was pleased to express herself in a late conversation with the Prince Dolgoroucki) to my cruelty. What the sex see in me I cannot conceive, but the Empress is not the only female sovereign who has offered me her hand.

Some people have very illiberally reported that Captain Phipps did not proceed as far as he might have done upon that expedition. Here it becomes my duty to acquit him; our ship was in a very proper trim till I loaded it with such an immense quantity of bear-skins and hams, after which it would have been madness to have attempted to proceed farther, as we

[1] Catherine II.

49

were now scarcely able to combat a brisk gale, much less those mountains of ice which lay in the higher latitudes.

The captain has since often expressed a dissatisfaction that he had no share in the honours of that day, which he emphatically called *bearskin-day*. He has also been very desirous of knowing by what art I destroyed so many thousands, without fatigue or danger to myself; indeed, he is so ambitious of dividing the glory with me, that we have actually quarrelled about it, and we are not now upon speaking terms. He boldly asserts I had no merit in deceiving the bears, because I was covered with one of their skins; nay, he declares there is not, in his opinion, in Europe, so complete a bear naturally, as himself among the human species.

He is now a noble peer, and I am too well acquainted with good manners to dispute so delicate a point with his lordship.

I omitted several very material parts in my father's journey across the English Channel to Holland, which, that they may not be totally lost, I will now faithfully give you in his own words, as I heard him relate them to his friends several times.

'On my arrival,' says my father, 'at Helvoetsluys, I was observed to breathe with some difficulty: upon the inhabitants inquiring into the cause, I informed them that the animal upon whose back I rode from Harwich across to their shore did not swim! Such is their peculiar form and disposition, that they cannot float or move upon the surface of the water; he ran with incredible swiftness upon the sands from shore to shore, driving fish in millions before him, many of which were quite different, from any I had yet seen, carrying their heads at the extremity of their tails. I crossed,' continued he, 'one prodigious range of rocks, equal in height to the Alps (the tops or highest, part of these marine mountains are said to be upwards of one hundred fathoms below the surface of the sea), on the sides of which there was a great variety of tall, noble trees, loaded with marine fruit, such as lobsters, crabs, oysters, scollops, mussels, cockles, &c., &c.; some of which were a cart-load singly! and none less than a porter's! All those which are brought on shore and sold in our markets are of an inferior dwarf kind, or, properly, waterfalls, i.e. fruit shook off the branches of the tree it grows upon by the motion of the water, as those in our gardens are by that of the wind! The lobster-trees appeared the richest, but the crab and oysters were the tallest. The periwinkle is a kind of shrub; it grows at the foot of the oyster-tree, and twines round it, as the ivy does the oak. I observed the effect of several accidents by shipwreck, &c., particularly a ship that had been wrecked by striking against a mountain or rock, the top of which lay within three fathoms of the surface. As she sunk she fell upon her side, and forced a very large lobster-tree out of its place. It was in the spring, when the lobsters were very young, and many of them being separated by the violence of the shock, they fell upon a crab-tree which was growing below them; they have, like the farina of plants, united, and produced a fish resembling both. I endeavoured to bring one with me, but it was too cumbersome, and my salt-water Pegasus seemed much displeased at every attempt to stop his career whilst I continued upon his back; besides, I was then, though galloping over a mountain of rocks that lay about midway along the passage, at least five hundred fathom below the surface of the sea, and began to find the want of air inconvenient; therefore I had no inclination to prolong the time. Add to this, my situation was in other respects very unpleasant; I met many large fish, who were, if I could judge by their open mouths, not only able, but really wished to devour us; now, as my Rosinante was blind, I had these hungry gentlemen's attempts to guard against, in addition to my other difficulties.

'As we drew near the Dutch shore, and the body of water over our heads did not exceed twenty fathoms, I thought I saw a human figure in a female dress then lying on the sand before me, with some signs of life; when I came close I perceived her hand move: I took it into mine, and brought her on shore as a corpse. An apothecary, who had just been instructed by Dr Hawes[1] (the Baron's father must have lived very lately if Dr Hawes was his preceptor), of London, treated her properly, and she recovered. She was the rib of a man who commanded a vessel belonging to Helvoetsluys. He was just going out of port on a voyage, when she, hearing he had got a mistress with him, followed him in an open boat. As soon as she had got on the quarter-deck, she flew at her husband, and attempted to strike him with such impetuosity, that he thought it most prudent to slip on one side, and let her make the impression of her fingers upon the waves rather than his face: he was not much out in his ideas of the consequence; for meeting no opposition, she went directly overboard, and it was my unfortunate lot to lay the foundation for bringing this happy pair together again.

'I can easily conceive what execrations the husband loaded me with, when, on his return, he found this gentle creature waiting his arrival, and learned the means by which she came

---

[1] William Hawes, M.D. (1736–1808) was a pioneer of artificial respiration and a founder of the Royal Humane Society for whose motto 'lateat scintillula forsan' he was responsible.

into the world again. However, great as the injury is which I have done this poor devil, I hope he will die in charity with me, as my motive was good, though the consequences to him are, it must be confessed, horrible.'

IV

TRAVELS IN CEYLON, SICILY, THE SOUTH SEAS AND ELSEWHERE

Some years before my beard announced approaching manhood, or, in other words, when I was neither man nor boy,[1] but between both, I expressed in repeated conversations a strong desire of seeing the world, from which I was discouraged by my parents, though my father had been no inconsiderable traveller himself, as will appear before I have reached the end of my singular, and, I may add, interesting adventures. A cousin, by my mother's side, took a liking to me, often said I was a fine forward youth, and was much inclined to gratify my curiosity. His eloquence had more effect than mine, for my father consented to my accompanying him in a voyage to the island of Ceylon, where his uncle had resided as governor many years.

We sailed from Amsterdam with dispatches from their High Mightinesses the States of Holland. The only circumstance which happened on our voyage worth relating, was the wonderful effects of a storm, which had torn up by the

[1] The reader's pardon is begged for this 'flashback'. Although it deals with the Baron's early youth, this adventure was prefixed to his earlier travels at a comparatively late date and is by some other hand than Raspe's.

roots a great number of trees of enormous bulk and height, in an island where we lay at anchor to take in wood and water; some of these trees weighed many tons, yet they were carried by the wind so amazingly high, that they appeared like the feathers of small birds floating in the air, for they were at least five miles above the earth: however, as soon as the storm subsided, they all fell perpendicularly into their respective places, and took root again, except the largest, which happened, when it was blown into the air, to have a man and his wife, a very honest old couple, upon its branches, gathering cucumbers (in this part of the globe, that useful vegetable grows upon trees); the weight of this couple, as the tree descended, over-balanced the trunk, and brought it down in a horizontal position: it fell upon the chief man of the island, and killed him on the spot; he had quitted his house in the storm, under an apprehension of its falling upon him, and was returning through his own garden when this fortunate accident happened. The word fortunate, here, requires some explanation. This chief was a man of a very avaricious and oppressive disposition, and though he had no family, the natives of the island were half-starved by his oppressive and infamous impositions.

The very goods which he had thus taken from them were spoiling in his stores, while the poor wretches from whom they were plundered were pining in poverty. Though the destruction of this tyrant was accidental, the people chose the cucumber-gatherers for their governors, as a mark of their gratitude for destroying, though accidentally, their late tyrant.

After we had repaired the damages we sustained in this remarkable storm, and taken leave of the new governor and his lady, we sailed with a fair wind for the object of our voyage.

In about six weeks we arrived at Ceylon, where we were received with great marks of friendship and true politeness. The following singular adventure may not prove unentertaining.

After we had resided at Ceylon about a fortnight, I accompanied one of the governor's brothers upon a shooting party. He was a strong, athletic man, and being used to that climate (for he had resided there some years), he bore the violent heat of the sun much better than I could; in our excursion he had made a considerable progress through a thick wood when I was only at the entrance.

Near the banks of a large piece of water, which had engaged my attention, I thought I heard a rustling noise behind; on turning about I was almost petrified (as who would not?) at the sight of a lion, which was evidently approaching with the intention of satisfying his appetite with my poor carcass, and that without asking my consent. What was to be done in this horrible dilemma? I had not even a moment for reflection; my piece was only charged with swan-shot, and I had no other about me: however, though I could have no idea of killing such an animal with that weak kind of ammunition, yet I had some hopes of frightening him by the report, and perhaps of wounding him also. I immediately let fly, without waiting till he was within reach; and the report did but enrage him, for he now quickened his pace, and seemed to approach me full speed: I attempted to escape, but that only added (if an addition could be made) to my distress; for the moment I turned about, I found a large crocodile, with his mouth extended almost ready to receive me; on my right hand was the piece of water before mentioned, and on my left a deep precipice, said to have, as I have since learned, a receptacle at the bottom for venomous creatures; in short, I gave myself up as lost, for the lion was now upon his hind-legs, just in the act of seizing me: I fell involuntarily to the ground with fear, and, as it afterwards appeared, he sprang over me. I lay some time in a situation which no language can describe, expecting to feel his teeth or talons in some part of me every moment: after waiting in this prostrate situation a few seconds, I heard a violent but unusual noise, different from any sound that had ever before assailed my ears; nor is it at all to be wondered at, when I inform you from whence it proceeded: after listening for some time, I ventured to raise my head and look round, when, to my unspeakable joy, I perceived the lion had, by the eagerness with which he sprung at me, jumped forward, as I fell, into the crocodile's mouth! which, as before observed, was wide open; the head of the one stuck in the throat of the other! and they were struggling to extricate themselves: I fortunately recollected my *couteau de chasse* which was by my side; with this instrument I severed the lion's head at one blow, and the body fell at my feet! I then, with the but-end of my fowling-piece, rammed the head farther into the throat of the crocodile, and destroyed him by suffocation, for he could neither gorge nor eject it.

Soon after I had thus gained a complete victory over my two powerful adversaries, my companion arrived in search of me; for, finding I did not follow him into the wood, he returned, apprehending I had lost my way, or met with some accident.

After mutual congratulations, we measured the crocodile, which was just forty feet in length.

As soon as we had related this extraordinary adventure to the governor, he sent a waggon and servants, who brought home the two carcases. The lion's skin was properly preserved, with its hair on; after which it was made into tobacco-pouches, and presented by me upon our return to Holland to the burgomasters, who in return, requested my acceptance of a thousand ducats.

The skin of the crocodile was stuffed in the usual manner, and makes a capital article in their public museum at Amsterdam, where the exhibitor relates the whole story to each spectator, with such additions as he thinks proper: some of his variations are rather extravagant; one of them is, that the lion jumped quite through the crocodile, and was making his escape at the back door, when as soon as his head appeared, Monsieur the Great Baron (as he is pleased to call me) cut it off, and three feet of the crocodile's tail along with it; nay, so little attention has this fellow to the truth, that he sometimes adds, as soon as the crocodile missed his tail, he turned about, snatched the *couteau de chasse* out of Monsieur's hand, and swallowed it with such eagerness, that it pierced his heart, and killed him immediately!

The little regard which this impudent knave has to veracity makes me sometimes apprehensive that my *real facts* may fall under suspicion, by being found in company with his confounded inventions.

In a voyage which I made to the East Indies with Captain Hamilton, I took a favourite pointer with me; he was, to use a common phrase, worth his weight in gold, for he never deceived me. One day when we were, by the best observations we could make, at least three hundred leagues from land, my dog pointed; I observed him for near an hour with astonishment, and mentioned the circumstance to the captain and every officer on board, asserting that we must be near land, for my dog smelt game. This occasioned a general laugh; but that did not alter in the least the good opinion I had of my dog. After much conversation pro and con, I boldly told the captain I placed more confidence in Tray's nose than I did in the eyes of every seaman on board, and therefore proposed laying the sum I had agreed to pay for my passage (viz., one hundred guineas), that we should find game within half an hour. The captain (a good, hearty fellow) laughed again, desired Mr Crawford the surgeon, who was present, to feel my pulse: he did so, and reported me in perfect health. The following dialogue between them took place; I overheard it, though spoken low, and at some distance.

Captain: His brain is turned; I cannot with honour accept his wager.

Surgeon: I am of a different opinion; he is quite sane, and depends more upon the scent of his dog, than he will upon the judgment of all the officers on board: he will certainly lose, and he richly merits it.

Captain: Such a wager cannot be fair on my side; however, I'll take him up, if I return his money afterwards.

During the above conversation Tray continued in the same situation, and confirmed me still more in my former opinion. I proposed the wager a second time, it was then accepted.

Done! and Done! were scarcely said on both sides, when some sailors who were fishing in the long-boat, which was made fast to the stern of the ship, harpooned an exceeding large shark, which they brought on board, and began to cut up for the purpose of barrelling the oil, when, behold, they found no less than *six brace of live partridges* in this animal's stomach!

They had been so long in that situation, that one of the hens was sitting upon four eggs, and a fifth was hatching when the shark was opened!!! This young bird we brought up by placing it with a litter of kittens that came into the world a few minutes before! The old cat was as fond of it as of any of her own four-legged progeny, and made herself very unhappy when it flew out of her reach till it returned again. As to the other partridges, there were four hens amongst them: one or more were, during the voyage, constantly sitting, and consequently we had plenty of game at the captain's table; and in gratitude to poor Tray (for being a means of winning one hundred guineas), I ordered him the bones daily, and sometimes a whole bird.

I have already informed you of one trip I made to the moon, in search of my silver hatchet: I afterwards made another in a much pleasanter manner, and staid in it long enough to take notice of several things, which I will endeavour to describe as accurately as my memory will permit.

I went on a voyage of discovery, at the request of a distant relation, who had a strange notion that there were people to be found equal in magnitude to those described by Gulliver in the empire of Brobdignag. For my part I always treated that account as fabulous; however, to oblige him, for he had made me his heir, I undertook it, and sailed for the South Seas, where we arrived without meeting with anything remarkable, except some flying men and women who were playing at leap-frog, and dancing minuets in the air.

On the eighteenth day after we had passed the Island of Otaheité[1], mentioned by Captain Cook as the place from whence they brought Omai, a hurricane blew our ship at least one thousand leagues above the surface of the water, and kept it at that height till a fresh gale arising, filled the sails in every part, and onwards we travelled at a prodigious rate; thus we proceeded above the clouds for six weeks. At last we discovered a great land in the sky, like a shining island, round and bright, where coming into a convenient harbour, we went on shore, and soon found it was inhabited. Below us we saw another earth, containing cities, trees, mountains, rivers, seas, &c., which we conjectured was this world which we had left. Here we saw huge figures riding upon vultures of a prodigious

[1] Otherwise Tahiti. Omai was brought to England by Captain Cook in his second voyage (1775).

size, and each of them having three heads. To form some idea of the magnitude of these birds, I must inform you, that each of their wings is as wide, and six times the length of the main sheet of our vessel, which was about six hundred tons burthen. Thus, instead of riding upon horses, as we do in this world, the inhabitants of the Moon (for we now found we were in madam Luna) fly about on these birds. The king, we found, was engaged in a war with the SUN, and he offered me a commission, but I declined the honour his majesty intended me.

Everything in *this* world is of extraordinary magnitude; a common flea being much larger than one of our sheep: in making war, their principal weapons are radishes, which are used as darts; those who are wounded by them, die immediately. Their shields are made of mushrooms, and their darts (when radishes are out of season) of the tops of asparagus. Some of the natives of the dog-star are to be seen here; commerce tempts them to ramble: their faces are like large mastiffs, with their eyes near the lower end or tip of their noses; they have no eyelids, but cover their eyes with the end of their tongues when they go to sleep: they are generally twenty feet high. As to the natives of the Moon, none of them are less in stature than thirty-six feet; they are not called the human species, but the cooking animals, for they all dress their food by fire, as we do, but lose no time at their meals, as they open their left side, and place the whole quantity at once in their stomach, then shut it again till the same day in the next month; for they never indulge themselves with food more than twelve times in a year, or once a month. All but gluttons and epicures must prefer this method to ours.

There is but one sex either of the cooking or any other

animals in the Moon; they are all produced from trees of various sizes and foliage: that which produces the cooking animal, or human species, is much more beautiful than any of the others; it has large straight boughs, and flesh-coloured leaves, and the fruit it produces are nuts or pods, with hard shells, at least two yards long: when they become ripe, which is known from their changing colour, they are gathered with great care, and laid by as long as they think proper: when they choose to animate the seed of these nuts, they throw them into a large cauldron of boiling water, which opens the shells in a few hours, and out jumps the creature.

Nature forms their minds for different pursuits before they come into the world; from one shell comes forth a warrior, from another a philosopher, from a third a divine, from a fourth a lawyer, from a fifth a farmer, from a sixth a clown, &c., &c., and each of them immediately begins to perfect themselves, by practising what they before knew only in theory.

When they grow old they do not die, but turn into air, and dissolve like smoke! As for their drink, they need none; the only evacuations they have are insensible, and by their breath. They have but one finger upon each hand, with which they perform everything in as perfect a manner as we who have four besides the thumb. Their heads are placed under their right arm; and, when they are going to travel, or about any violent exercise, they generally leave them at home, for they can consult them at any distance; this is a very common practice: and when those of rank or quality among the Lunarians have an inclination to see what's going forward among the common people, they stay at home, i.e. the body stays at home, and sends the head only, which is suffered to be present incog. and return at pleasure with an account of what has passed.

The stones of their grapes are exactly like hail; and I am perfectly satisfied that when a storm or high wind in the Moon shakes their vines, and breaks the grapes from the stalks, the stones fall down and form our hail showers. I would advise those who are of my opinion, to save a quantity of these stones when it hails next, and make Lunarian wine. It is common beverage at St Luke's. Some material circumstances I had nearly omitted. They put their bellies to the same use as we do a sack, and throw whatever they have occasion for into it, for they can shut and open it again when they please, as they do their stomachs: they are not troubled with bowels, liver, heart, or any other intestines, neither are they encumbered with clothes, nor is there any part of their bodies unseemly or indecent to exhibit.

Their eyes they can take in and out of their places when they please, and can see as well with them in their hand as in their head! and if by any accident they lose or damage one, they can borrow or purchase another, and see as clearly with it as their own. Dealers in eyes are on that account very numerous in most parts of the Moon, and in this article alone all the inhabitants are whimsical: sometimes green and sometimes yellow eyes are the fashion. I know these things appear strange; but if the shadow of a doubt can remain on any person's mind, I say, let him take a voyage there himself, and then he will know I am a traveller of veracity.

My first visit to England was about the beginning of the present King's reign. I had occasion to go down to Wapping, to see some goods shipped, which I was sending to some friends at Hamburgh: after that business was over, I took the

Tower Wharf in my way back. Here I found the sun very
powerful; and I was so much fatigued that I stepped into one
of the cannon to compose me, where I fell fast asleep. This
was about noon; it was the fourth of June; exactly at one
o'clock these cannon were all discharged in memory of the
day. They had been all charged that morning, and having no
suspicion of my situation, I was shot over the houses on the
opposite side of the river, into a farmer's yard, between
Bermondsey and Deptford, where I fell upon a large hay-
stack, without waking, and continued there in a sound sleep
till hay became so extravagantly dear (which was about three
months after), that the farmer found it his interest to send his
whole stock to market: the stack I was reposing upon was the
largest in the yard, containing above five hundred load; they
began to cut that first. I waked (with the voices of the people

who had ascended the ladders to begin at the top), and got up, totally ignorant of my situation; in attempting to run away I fell upon the farmer to whom the hay belonged, and broke his neck, yet received no injury myself! I afterwards found, to my great consolation, that this fellow was a most detestable character, always keeping the produce of his grounds for extravagant markets.

Mr Brydone's Travels to Sicily[1], which I had read with great pleasure, induced me to pay a visit to Mount Etna; my voyage to this place was not attended with any circumstances worth relating. One morning early, three or four days after my arrival, I set out from a cottage where I had slept, within six miles of the foot of the mountain, determined to explore the internal parts, if I perished in the attempt. After three hours hard labour I found myself at the top; it was then, and had been for upwards of three weeks, raging; its appearance in this state has been so frequently noticed by different travellers, that I will not tire you with descriptions of objects you are already acquainted with. I walked round the edge of the crater, which appeared to be fifty times at least as capacious as the Devil's Punch-Bowl near Petersfield, on the Portsmouth Road, but not so broad at the bottom, as in that part it resembles the contracted part of a funnel more than a punch-bowl. At last, having made up my mind, in I sprang feet foremost: I soon found myself in a warm berth, and my body bruised and burnt in various parts by the red-hot cinders, which, by their violent ascent, opposed my descent; however, my weight soon brought me to the bottom, where I found myself in the

[1] Patrick Brydone, *Tour Through Sicily*. See Introduction.

midst of noise and clamour, mixed with the most horrid imprecations; after recovering my senses, and feeling a reduction of my pain, I began to look about me. Guess, gentlemen, my astonishment, when I found myself in the company of Vulcan and his cyclops, who had been quarrelling, for the three weeks before mentioned, about the observation of good order and due subordination, and which had occasioned such alarms for that space of time in the world above. However, my arrival restored peace to the whole society, and Vulcan himself did me the honour of applying plasters to my wounds, which healed them immediately; he also placed refreshments before me, particularly nectar, and other rich wines, such as the gods and goddesses only aspire to. After this repast was over Vulcan ordered Venus to show me every indulgence which my situation required. To describe the apartment and the couch on which I reposed, is totally impossible, therefore I will not attempt it: let it suffice to say, it exceeds the power of language to do it justice, or speak of that kind-hearted goddess in any terms equal to her merit.

Vulcan gave me a very concise account of Mount Etna; he said it was nothing more than an accumulation of ashes thrown from his forge; that he was frequently obliged to chastise his people, at whom, in his passion he made it a practice to throw red-hot coals at home, which they often parried with great dexterity, and then threw them up into the world, to place them out of his reach, for they never attempted to assault him in return, by throwing them back again: 'our quarrels,' added he, 'last sometimes three or four months, and these appearances of coals or cinders in the world are what I find you mortals call eruptions.' Mount Vesuvius, he assured me, was another of his shops, to which he had a passage three hundred and fifty leagues under the bed of the sea, where similar quarrels produced similar eruptions. I should have continued here as an humble attendant upon Madam Venus, but some busy tattlers, who delight in mischief, whispered a tale in Vulcan's ear, which roused in him a fit of jealousy not to be appeased. Without the least previous notice he took me one morning under his arm, as I was waiting upon Venus, agreeable to custom, and carried me to an apartment I had never before seen, in which there was, to all appearance, a *well* with a wide mouth: over this he held me at arm's length, and saying, '*Ungrateful mortal, return to the world from whence you came,*' without giving me the least opportunity of reply, dropped me in the centre. I found myself descending with an increasing rapidity, till the horror of my mind deprived me of all reflection. I suppose I fell into a trance; from which I was suddenly roused, by plunging into a large body of water illuminated by the rays of the sun!

I could, from my infancy, swim well, and play tricks in the water. I now found myself in paradise, considering the horrors of mind I had just been released from. After looking about me some time, I could discover nothing but an expanse of sea, extending beyond the eye in every direction; I also found it very cold, a different climate from Master Vulcan's shop. At last I observed at some distance, a body of amazing magnitude, like a huge rock, approaching me: I soon discovered it to be a piece of floating ice; I swam round it till I found a place where I could ascend to the top, which I did, but not without some difficulty. Still I was out of sight of land, and despair returned with double force: however, before night came on, I saw a sail, which we approached very fast; when it was within a very small distance I hailed them in German; they answered in Dutch; I then flung myself into the sea, and they threw out a rope, by which I was taken on board. I now inquired where we were, and was informed, in the great Southern Ocean; this opened a discovery which removed all my doubts and difficulties. It was now evident that I had passed from Mount Etna through the centre of the earth to the South Seas; this, gentlemen, was a much shorter cut than going round the world, and which no man has accomplished, or ever attempted, but myself: however, the next time I perform it, I will be much more particular in my observations.

I took some refreshment, and went to rest. The Dutch are a very rude sort of people; I related the Etna passage to the officers, exactly as I have done to you; and some of them, particularly the Captain, seemed by his grimace and half-sentences to doubt my veracity: however, as he had kindly taken me on board his vessel, and was then in the very act of administering to my necessities, I pocketed the affront.

I now in my turn began to inquire where they were bound? To which they answered, they were in search of new discoveries; 'and if,' said they, 'your story is true, a new passage is really discovered, and we shall not return disappointed.' We were now exactly in Captain Cook's first track, and arrived the next morning in Botany Bay. This place I would by no means recommend to the English government as a receptacle for felons, or place of punishment: it should rather be the reward of merit, nature having most bountifully bestowed her best gifts upon it.

We staid here but three days; the fourth after our departure a most dreadful storm arose, which in a few hours destroyed all our sails, splintered our bowsprit, and brought down our topmast; it fell directly upon the box that enclosed our compass, which, with the compass, was broken to pieces. Every one who has been at sea knows the consequences of such a misfortune; we now were at a loss where to steer. At length the storm abated, which was followed by a steady brisk gale, that carried us at least forty knots an hour for six months! when we began to observe an amazing change in everything about us; our spirits became light, our noses were regaled with the most aromatic effluvia imaginable: the sea had also changed its complexion, and from green became white !! Soon after these wonderful alterations we saw land, and not at any great distance an inlet, which we sailed up near sixty leagues, and found it wide and deep, flowing with milk of the most delicious taste. Here we landed, and soon found it was an island consisting of one large cheese: we discovered this by one of the company fainting away as soon as we landed; this man always had an aversion to cheese: when he recovered, he desired the cheese to be taken from under his feet; upon examination we found him perfectly right, for the whole island, as before observed, was nothing but a cheese of immense magnitude! Upon this the inhabitants, who are amazingly numerous, principally sustain themselves, and it grows every night in proportion as it is consumed in the day. Here seemed to be plenty of vines, with bunches of large grapes, which, upon being pressed, yielded nothing but milk. We saw the inhabitants running races upon the surface of the milk; they were upright, comely figures, nine feet high, have three legs, and but one arm; upon the whole, their form was graceful, and when they quarrel, they exercise a straight horn, which grows in adults from the centre of their foreheads, with great adroitness: they did not sink at all, but ran and walked upon the surface of the milk, as we do upon a bowling-green.

Upon this island of cheese grows great plenty of corn, the ears of which produce loaves of bread, ready made, of a round form like mushrooms. We discovered, in our rambles over this cheese, seventeen other rivers of milk, and ten of wine.

After thirty-eight days' journey we arrived on the opposite side to that on which we landed; here we found some blue mould, as cheese-eaters call it, from whence spring all kinds of rich fruit: instead of breeding mites it produced peaches, nectarines, apricots, and a thousand delicious fruits, which we are not acquainted with. In these trees, which are of an amazing size, were plenty of birds' nests; amongst others was a kingfisher's of prodigious magnitude; it was at least twice the circumference of the dome of St Paul's Church in London. Upon inspection, this nest was made of huge trees, curiously joined together; there were, let me see (*for I make it a rule always to speak within compass*), there were upwards of five hundred eggs in this nest, and each of them was as large as four common hogsheads or eight barrels, and we could not only see, but hear the young ones chirping within. Having, with great fatigue, cut open one of these eggs, we let out a young one unfeathered, considerably larger than twenty full-grown vultures. Just as we had given this youngster his liberty, the old kingfisher lighted, and seizing our captain, who had been active in breaking the egg, in one of her claws, flew with him above a mile high, and then let him drop into the sea, but not till she had beaten all his teeth out of his mouth with her wings.

Dutchmen generally swim well; he soon joined us, and we retreated to our ship. On our return we took a different route, and observed many strange objects. We shot two wild oxen, each with one horn, also like the inhabitants, except that it sprouted from between the eyes of these animals: we were afterwards concerned at having destroyed them, as we found, by inquiry, they tamed these creatures, and used them as we do horses, to ride upon and draw their carriages; their flesh, we were informed, is excellent, but useless where people live upon cheese and milk. When we had reached within two days' journey of the ship we observed three men hanging to a tall tree by the heels: upon inquiring the cause of their punishment, I found they had all been travellers, and upon their return home had deceived their friends, by describing places they never saw, and relating things that never happened: this gave me no concern, *as I have ever confined myself to facts.*

As soon as we arrived at the ship, we unmoored, and set sail from this extraordinary country, when, to our astonishment, all the trees upon shore, of which there were a great number very tall and large, paid their respects to us twice, bowing to exact time, and immediately recovered their former posture, which was quite erect.

By what we could learn of this CHEESE, it was considerably larger than the continent of all Europe!

After sailing three months we knew not where, being still without compass, we arrived in a sea which appeared to be almost black; upon tasting it, we found it most excellent wine, and had great difficulty to keep the sailors from getting drunk with it: however, in a few hours we found ourselves surrounded by whales and other animals of an immense magnitude; one of which appeared to be too large for the eye to form a judgment of: we did not see him till we were close to him. This monster drew our ship, with all her masts standing, and sails bent, by suction into its mouth, between its teeth, which were much larger and taller than the mast of a first-rate man-of-war. After we had been in his mouth some time, he opened it pretty wide, took in an immense quantity of water, and floated our vessel, which was at least 500 tons burthen, into his stomach; here we lay as quiet as at anchor in a dead calm. The air, to be sure, was rather warm, and very offensive. We found anchors, cables, boats and barges in abundance, and a considerable number of ships, some laden and some not, which the creature had swallowed. Everything was transacted by torch-light; no sun, no moon, no planet, to make observations from. We were all generally afloat and aground twice a-day: whenever he drank, it became high water with us; and when he evacuated, we found ourselves aground: upon a moderate computation, he took in more water at a single draught than is generally to be found in the Lake of Geneva, though that is above thirty miles in circumference. On the second day of our confinement in these regions of darkness, I ventured at low water, as we called it, when the ship was aground, to ramble with the Captain, and a few of the other officers, with lights in our hands: we met with people of all nations, to the amount of upwards of ten thousand; they were going to hold a council how to recover their liberty; some of them having lived in this animal's stomach several years, there were several children here who had never seen the world, their mothers having lain in repeatedly in this warm situation. Just as the chairman was going to inform us of the business upon which we were assembled, this plaguy fish, becoming thirsty, drank in his usual manner: the water poured in with such impetuosity, that we were all obliged to retreat to our respective ships immediately, or run the risque of being drowned; some were obliged to swim for it, and with difficulty saved their lives. In a few hours after, we were more fortunate; we met again just after the monster had evacuated. I was chosen chairman, and the first thing I did was to propose splicing two main-masts together; and the next time he opened his mouth, to be ready to wedge them in, so as to prevent his shutting it. It was unanimously approved. One hundred stout men were chosen upon this service. We had scarcely got our masts properly prepared, when an opportunity offered; the monster opened his mouth, immediately the top of the mast was placed against the roof, and the other end pierced his tongue, which effectually prevented him from shutting his mouth. As soon as everything in his stomach was afloat, we manned a few boats, who rowed themselves and us into the world. The daylight, after, as near as we could judge, three months' confinement in total darkness, cheered our spirits surprisingly. When we had all taken our leave of this capacious animal, we mustered just a fleet of ninety-five ships, of all nations, who had been in this confined situation.

We left the two masts in his mouth, to prevent others being confined in the same horrid gulph of darkness and filth. Our first object was to learn what part of the world we were in: this we were for some time at a loss to ascertain; at last I found, from former observations, that we were in the Caspian Sea! which washes part of the country of the Calmuck Tartars. How we came here it was impossible to conceive, as this sea has no communication with any other. One of the inhabitants of the Cheese Island, whom I had brought with me, accounted for it thus: that the monster in whose stomach we had been so long confined had carried us here through some subterraneous passage; however, we pushed to shore, and I was the first who landed. Just as I put my foot upon the ground a large bear leaped upon me with his fore-paws; I caught one in each hand, and squeezed him till he cried out most lustily; however, in this position I held him till I starved him to death. You may laugh, gentlemen, but this was soon accomplished, as I prevented him licking his paws. From hence I travelled up to St Petersburgh a second time; here an old friend gave me a most excellent pointer, descended from the famous bitch before mentioned, that littered while she was hunting a hare. I had the misfortune to have him shot soon after by a blundering sportsman, who fired at him instead of a covey of partridges which he had just set. Of this creature's skin I have had this waistcoat made (showing his waistcoat) which always leads me involuntarily to game if I walk in the fields in the proper season; and when I come within shot, *one of the buttons constantly flies off, and lodges upon the spot where the sport is*; and as the birds rise, being always primed and cocked, I never miss them. Here are now but three buttons left. I shall have a new set sewed on against the shooting season commences.

When a covey of partridges is disturbed in this manner, by the button falling amongst them, they always rise from the ground in a direct line before each other. I one day, by forgetting to take my ramrod out of my gun, shot it straight through a leash, as regularly as if the cook had spitted them. I had forgot to put in any shot, and the rod had been made so hot with the powder, that the birds were completely roasted by the time I reached home.

74

Since my arrival in England I have accomplished what I had very much at heart, viz. providing for the inhabitant of the Cheese Island, whom I had brought with me. My old friend, Sir William Chambers,[1] who is entirely indebted to me for all his ideas of Chinese gardening, by a description of which he has gained such high reputation; I say, gentlemen, in a discourse which I had with this gentleman, he seemed much distressed for a contrivance to light the lamps at the new buildings, Somerset House; the common mode with ladders, he observed, was both dirty and inconvenient. My native of the Cheese Island popped into my head; he was only nine feet high when I first brought him from his own country, but was now increased to ten and a half: I introduced him to Sir William, and he is appointed to that honourable office. He is also to carry, under a large cloak, an utensil in each coat pocket, instead of those four which Sir William has *very properly* fixed for private purposes in so conspicuous a situation, the great quadrangle.

He has also obtained from Mr Pitt the situation of messenger to his Majesty's lords of the bed-chamber, whose principal employment will *now* be, divulging the secrets of the Royal household to their *worthy* Patron.

About the beginning of his present Majesty's reign I had some business with a distant relation who then lived on the Isle of Thanet; it was a family dispute, and not likely to be finished soon. I made it a practice during my residence there, the weather being fine, to walk out every morning. After a

[1] Sir William Chambers, R.A. (1726–1796). The architect, among other public buildings, of Somerset House (1786).

few of these excursions, I observed an object upon a great eminence about three miles distant; I extended my walk to it, and found the ruins of an ancient temple: I approached it with admiration and astonishment; the traces of grandeur and magnificence which yet remained were evident proofs of its former splendour: here I could not help lamenting the ravages and devastations of time, of which that once noble structure exhibited such a melancholy proof. I walked round it several times, meditating on the fleeting and transitory nature of all terrestrial things: on the eastern end were the remains of a lofty tower, near forty feet high, overgrown with ivy, the top apparently flat; I surveyed it on every side very minutely, thinking that if I could gain its summit, I should enjoy the most delightful prospect of the circumjacent country. Animated with this hope, I resolved, if possible, to gain the summit; which I at length effected by means of the ivy, though not without great difficulty and danger: the top I found covered with this evergreen, except a large chasm in the middle. After I had surveyed with pleasing wonder the beauties of art and nature that conspired to enrich the scene, curiosity prompted me to sound the opening in the middle, in order to ascertain its depth, as I entertained a suspicion that it might probably communicate with some unexplored sub-terranean cavern in the hill; but having no line, I was at a loss how to proceed. After revolving the matter in my thoughts for some time, I resolved to drop a stone down and listen to the echo: having found one that answered my purpose, I placed myself over the hole, with one foot on each side, and stooping down to listen, I dropped the stone; which I had no sooner done than I heard a rustling below, and suddenly a monstrous eagle put up its head right opposite my face; and rising up with irresistible force, carried me away seated on its shoulders. I instantly grasped it round the neck, which was large enough to fill my arms; and its wings, when extended, were ten yards from one extremity to the other. As it rose with a regular ascent, my seat was perfectly easy, and I enjoyed the prospect below with inexpressible pleasure. It hovered over Margate for some time, was seen by several people, and many shots were fired at it; one ball hit the heel of my shoe, but did me no injury. It then directed its course to Dover cliff, where it alighted, and I thought of dismounting; but was prevented by a sudden discharge of musquetry from a party of marines that were exercising on the beach: the balls flew about my head, and rattled on the feathers of the eagle like hail-stones; yet I could not perceive it had received any injury. It instantly reascended and flew over the sea towards Calais; but so very high that the Channel seemed to be no broader than the Thames at London Bridge. In a quarter of an hour I found myself over a thick wood in France, where the eagle descended very rapidly, which caused me to slip down to the back part of its head; but alighting on a large tree, and raising its head, I recovered my seat as before, but saw no possibility of disengaging myself without the danger of being killed by the fall: so I determined to sit fast, thinking it would carry me to the Alps, or some other high mountain, where I could dismount without any danger. After resting a few minutes it took wing, flew several times round the wood, and screamed loud enough to be heard across the English Channel. In a few minutes one of the same species arose out of the wood, and flew directly towards us: it surveyed me with evident marks of displeasure, and came very near me. After flying several times round, they both directed their course to the south-west. I soon observed that the one I rode upon could not keep pace with the other, but inclined towards the earth, on account of my weight; its companion perceiving this, turned round and placed itself in such a position that the other could rest its head on its rump: in this manner they proceeded till noon, when I saw the rock of Gibraltar very distinctly. The day being clear, notwithstanding my degree of elevation, the earth's surface appeared just like a map, where land, sea, lakes, rivers, mountains, and the like, were perfectly distinguishable; and having some knowledge of geography, I was at no loss to determine what part of the globe I was in.

Whilst I was contemplating this wonderful prospect a dreadful howling suddenly began all around me, and in a moment I was invested by thousands of small black, deformed, frightful-looking creatures, who pressed me on all sides in such a manner that I could neither move hand or foot: but I had not been in their possession more than ten minutes when I heard the most delightful music that can possibly be imagined; which was suddenly changed into a noise the most awful and tremendous, to which the report of cannon, or the loudest claps of thunder could bear no more proportion than the gentle zephyrs of the evening to the most dreadful hurricane: but the shortness of its duration prevented all those fatal effects which a prolongation of it would certainly have been attended with.

The music commenced, and I saw a great number of the most beautiful little creatures seize the other party, and throw them with great violence into something like a snuff-box, which they shut down; and one threw it away with incredible velocity; then turning to me, he said, they whom he had secured were a party of devils, who had wandered from their proper habitation; and that the vehicle in which they were enclosed would fly with unabating rapidity for ten thousand years, when it would burst of its own accord, and the devils would recover their liberty and faculties, as at the present moment. He had no sooner finished this relation than the music ceased, and they all disappeared, leaving me in a state of mind bordering on the confines of despair.

When I had recomposed myself a little, and looking before me with inexpressible pleasure, I observed that the eagles were preparing to light on the peak of Teneriffe: they descended on the top of a rock; but seeing no possible means of escape if I dismounted, determined me to remain where I was. The eagles sat down seemingly fatigued, when the heat of the sun soon caused them both to fall asleep; nor did I long resist its fascinating power. In the cool of the evening, when the sun had retired below the horizon, I was roused from sleep by the eagle moving under me; and having stretched myself along its back, I sat up, and reassumed my travelling position, when they both took wing, and having placed themselves as before, directed their course to South America. The moon shining bright during the whole night, I had a fine view of all the islands in those seas.

About the break of day we reached the great continent of America, that part called Terra Firma, and descended on the top of a very high mountain. At this time the moon, far distant in the west, and obscured by dark clouds, but just afforded light sufficient for me to discover a kind of shrubbery all around, bearing fruit something like cabbages, which the eagles began to feed on very eagerly. I endeavoured to discover my situation, but fogs and passing clouds involved me in the thickest darkness; and what rendered the scene still more shocking was the tremendous howling of wild beasts some of which appeared to be very near: however, I determined to keep my seat, imagining that the eagle would carry me away if any of them should make a hostile attempt. When daylight began to appear, I thought of examining the fruit which I had seen the eagles eat; and as some was hanging which I could easily come at, I took out my knife and cut a slice; but how great was my surprise to see that it had all the appearance of roast beef regularly mixed, both fat and lean! I tasted it, and found it well flavoured and delicious; then cut several large slices and put in my pocket, where I found a crust of bread which I had brought from Margate; took it out, and found three musket-balls that had been lodged in it on Dover cliff. I extracted them, and cutting a few slices more, made a hearty meal of bread and cold beef fruit. I then cut down two of the largest that grew near me, and tying them together with one of my garters, hung them over the eagle's neck for another occasion, filling my pockets at the same time. While I was settling these affairs, I observed a large fruit like an inflated bladder, which I wished to try an experiment upon; and striking my knife into one of them, a fine pure liquor like Hollands gin gushed out, which the eagles observing, eagerly drank up from the ground. I cut down the bladder as fast as I could, and saved about half a pint in the bottom of it, which I tasted, and could not distinguish it from the best mountain wine. I drank it all, and found myself greatly refreshed. By this time the eagles began to stagger against the shrubs. I endeavoured to keep my seat, but was soon thrown to some distance among the bushes. In attempting to rise, I put my hand upon a large hedgehog, which happened to lie among the grass upon its back: it instantly closed round my hand, so that I found it impossible to shake it off. I struck it several times against the ground without effect; but while I was thus employed I heard a rustling among the shrubbery, and looking up, I saw a huge animal within three yards of me: I could make no defence, but held out both my hands, when it rushed upon me, and seized that on which the hedgehog was fixed. My hand being soon relieved, I ran to some distance, where I saw the creature suddenly drop down, and expire with the hedgehog in its throat. When the danger was past I went to view the eagles, and found them lying on the grass fast asleep, being intoxicated with the liquor they had drank. Indeed I found myself considerably elevated by it, and seeing everything quiet, I began to search for some more, which I soon found; and having cut down two large bladders, about a gallon each, I tied them together, and hung them over the neck of the other eagle; and two smaller ones I tied with a cord round my own waist. Having secured a good stock of provisions, and perceiving the eagles begin to recover, I again took my seat. In half an hour they arose majestically from the place, without taking the least notice of their incumbrance. Each reassumed its former station; and directing their course to the northward, they crossed the Gulf of Mexico, entered North America, and steered directly for the Polar regions; which gave me the finest opportunity of viewing this vast continent that can possibly be imagined.

Before we entered the frigid zone the cold began to affect me; but piercing one of my bladders, I took a draught, and found that it could make no impression on me afterwards. Passing over Hudson's Bay, I saw several of the company's ships lying at anchor, and many tribes of Indians marching with their furs to market.

By this time I was so reconciled to my seat, and become such an expert rider, that I could sit up and look around me; but in general I lay along the eagle's neck, grasping it in my arms, with my hands immersed in its feathers, in order to keep them warm.

In these cold climates I observed that the eagles flew with greater rapidity, in order, I suppose, to keep their blood in circulation. In passing Baffin's Bay I saw several large Greenlandmen to the eastward, and many surprising mountains of ice in those seas.

While I was surveying these wonders of nature, it occurred to me that this was a good opportunity to discover the northwest passage, if any such thing existed, and not only obtain the reward offered by government, but the honour of a discovery pregnant with so many advantages to every European nation. But while my thoughts were absorbed in this pleasing reverie, I was alarmed by the first eagle striking its head against a solid transparent substance; and in a moment that which I rode experienced the same fate; and both fell down seemingly dead.

Here our lives must inevitably have terminated, had not a sense of danger, and the singularity of my situation, inspired me with a degree of skill and dexterity, which enabled us to fall near two miles perpendicular with as little inconveniency as if we had been let down with a rope: for no sooner did I perceive the eagles strike against a frozen cloud, which is very common near the poles, than (they being close together) I laid myself along the back of the foremost, and took hold of its wings to keep them extended, at the same time stretching out my legs behind to support the wings of the other. This had the desired effect; and we descended very safe on a mountain of ice, which I supposed to be about three miles above the level of the sea.

I dismounted; unloaded the eagles; opened one of the bladders, and administered some of the liquor to each of them, without once considering that the horrors of destruction seemed to have conspired against me. The roaring of waves, crashing of ice, and the howling of bears, conspired to form a scene the most awful and tremendous; but notwithstanding this, my concern for the recovery of the eagles was so great, that I was insensible of the danger to which I was exposed. Having rendered them every assistance in my power, I stood over them in painful anxiety, fully sensible that it was only by means of them that I could possibly be delivered from these abodes of despair.

But suddenly a monstrous bear began to roar behind me, with a voice like thunder. I turned round, and seeing the creature just ready to devour me, having the bladder of liquor in my hands, through fear I squeezed it so hard, that it burst, and the liquor flying in the eyes of the animal, totally deprived it of sight. It instantly turned from me, ran away in a state of distraction, and soon fell over a precipice of ice into the sea, where I saw it no more.

The danger being over, I again turned my attention to the eagles, whom I found in a fair way of recovery; and suspecting that they were faint for want of victuals, I took one of the beef

fruits, cut it into small slices, and presented them with it, which they devoured with avidity.

Having given them plenty to eat and drink, and disposed of the remainder of my provision, I took possession of my seat as before. After composing myself, and adjusting everything in the best manner, I began to eat and drink very heartily; and through the effects of the mountain, as I called it, was very cheerful, and began to sing a few verses of a song, which I had learned when I was a boy: but the noise soon alarmed the eagles, who had been asleep, through the quantity of liquor which they drank, and they arose seemingly much terri-fied. Happily for me, however, when I was feeding them I had accidentally turned their heads towards the south-east, which course they pursued with a rapid motion. In a few hours I saw the western isles, and soon after had the inexpressible pleasure of seeing Old England. I took no notice of the seas or islands over which I passed.

The eagles descended gradually as they drew near the shore, intending, as I supposed, to alight on one of the Welch moun-tains; but when they came to the distance of about sixty yards, two guns were fired at them, loaded with balls, one of which took place in a bladder of liquor that hung to my waist; the other entered the breast of the foremost eagle, who fell to the ground, while that which I rode, having received no injury, flew away with amazing swiftness.

This circumstance alarmed me exceedingly, and I began to think it was impossible for me to escape with my life; but recovering a little, I once more looked down upon the earth; when, to my inexpressible joy, I saw Margate at a little dis-tance, and the eagle descending on the old tower whence it had carried me on the morning of the day before. It no sooner came down than I threw myself off, happy to find that I was once more restored to the world. The eagle flew away in a few minutes, and I sat down to compose my fluttering spirits, which I did in a few hours.

I soon paid a visit to my friends, and related these adventures. Amazement stood in every countenance; their congratulations on my returning in safety were repeated with an unaffected degree of pleasure, and we passed the evening as we are doing now, every person present paying the highest compliments to my COURAGE and VERACITY.

A SEQUEL TO
THE ADVENTURES OF BARON MUNCHAUSEN

Humbly Dedicated

to

MR BRUCE

THE ABYSSINIAN TRAVELLER

*As the Baron conceives that it may be of some service
to him, previous to his making another expedition
into Abyssinia: but if this advice does not
please Mr Bruce, the Baron is willing to
fight him on any terms he pleases.*

PREFACE

Baron Munchausen has certainly been productive of much benefit to the literary world; the numbers of egregious travellers have been such, that they demanded a very Gulliver to surpass them. If Baron de Tott dauntlessly discharged an enormous piece of artillery, the Baron Munchausen has done more; he has taken it and swam with it across the sea. When travellers are solicitous to be the heroes of their own story, surely they must admit to superiority, and blush at seeing themselves out-done by the renowned Munchausen: I doubt whether any one hitherto, Pantagruel, Gargantua, Captain Lemuel, or De Tott, has been able to out-do our Baron in this species of excellence: and as at present our curiosity seems much directed to the interior of Africa, it must be edifying to have the real relation of Munchausen's adventures there before any further intelligence arrives; for he seems to adapt himself and his exploits to the spirit of the times, and recounts what he thinks should be most interesting to his auditors.

I do not say that the Baron, in the following stories, means a satire on any political matters whatever. No; but if the reader understands them so, I cannot help it.[1]

If the Baron meets with a parcel of negro ships carrying whites into slavery to work upon their plantations in a cold climate, should we therefore imagine that he intends a reflection on the present traffic in human flesh? And that, if the

[1] Though Bruce is the ostensible target of the *Sequel*, the range of topicalities is wide. The references are to events current rather later than those touched on in preceding sections, and are very much more numerous. Some are obvious, some obscure, some perhaps altogether irretrievable. Unearthing them provides literary and historical amusement of which I will not deprive the well-informed reader.—ED.

negroes should do so, it would be simple justice, as retaliation is the law of God! If we were to think this a reflection on any present commercial or political matter, we should be tempted to imagine, perhaps, some political ideas conveyed in every page, in every sentence of the whole. Whether such things are or are not the intentions of the Baron the reader must judge.

We have had not only wonderful travellers in this vile world, but splenetic travellers, and of these not a few, and also conspicuous enough. It is a pity, therefore, that the Baron has not endeavoured to surpass them also in this species of story-telling. Who is it can read the travels of Smellfungus, as Sterne calls him, without admiration? To think that a person from the North of Scotland should travel through some of the finest countries in Europe, and find fault with everything he meets—nothing to please him! And therefore, methinks, the Tour to the Hebrides is more excusable, and also perhaps Mr Twiss's Tour in Ireland. Dr Johnson, bred in the luxuriance of London, with more reason should become cross and splenetic in the bleak and dreary regions of the Hebrides.

The Baron, in the following work, seems to be sometimes philosophical; his account of the language of the interior of Africa, and its analogy with that of the inhabitants of the moon, shows him to be profoundly versed in the etymological antiquities of nations, and throws new light upon the abstruse history of the ancient Scythians, and the Collectanea.

His endeavour to abolish the custom of eating live flesh in the interior of Africa, as described in Bruce's Travels, is truly humane. But far be it from me to suppose, that by Gog and Magog and the Lord Mayor's show he means a satire upon any person or body of persons whatever: or, by a tedious litigated trial of blind judges and dumb matrons following a wild goose chase all round the world, he should glance at any trial whatever.

Nevertheless, I must allow that it was extremely presumptuous in Munchausen to tell half the sovereigns of the world that they were wrong, and advise them what they ought to do; and that instead of ordering millions of their subjects to massacre one another, it would be more to their interest to employ their forces in concert for the general good; as if he knew better than the Empress of Russia, the Grand Vizier, Prince Potemkin, or any other butcher in the world. But that he should be a royal Aristocrat, and take the part of the injured Queen of France in the present political drama, I am not at all surprised; but I suppose his mind was fired by reading the pamphlet written by Mr Burke.

CHAPTER I

*The Baron insists on the veracity of his former Memoirs—
Forms a design of making discoveries in the interior parts
of Africa—His discourse with Hilaro Frosticos about it—
His conversation with Lady Fragrantia—The Baron goes,
with other persons of distinction, to Court; relates an
anecdote of the Marquis de Bellecourt*

All that I have related before, said the Baron, is gospel; and
if there be any one so hardy as to deny it, I am ready to
fight him with any weapon he pleases. Yes, cried he, in a more
elevated tone, as he started from his seat, I will condemn him
to swallow this decanter, glass and all perhaps, and filled with
kerren-wasser [a kind of ardent spirit distilled from cherries,
and much used in some parts of Germany]. Therefore, my
dear friends and companions, have confidence in what I say,
and pay honour to the tales of Munchausen. A traveller has a
right to relate and embellish his adventures as he pleases, and
it is very unpolite to refuse that deference and applause they
deserve.

Having passed some time in England since the completion
of my former memoirs, I at length began to revolve in my
mind what a prodigious field of discovery must be in the
interior part of Africa. I could not sleep with the thoughts of
it; I therefore determined to gain every proper assistance from
Government to penetrate the celebrated source of the Nile,
and assume the viceroyship of the interior kingdoms of Africa,
or, at least, the great realm of Monomotapa. It was happy for
me that I had one most powerful friend at court, whom I shall
call the illustrious Hilaro Frosticos. You perchance know him

not by that name; but we had a language among ourselves, as well we may, for in the course of my peregrinations I have acquired precisely nine hundred and ninety-nine leash of languages. What! gentlemen, do you stare? Well, I allow there are not so many languages spoken in this vile world; but then, have I not been in the moon? and trust me, whenever I write a treatise upon education, I shall delineate methods of inculcating whole dozens of languages at once, French, Spanish, Greek, Hebrew, Cherokee, &c. in such a style as will shame all the pedagogues existing.

Having passed a whole night without being able to sleep for the vivid imagination of African discoveries, I hastened to the levee of my illustrious friend Hilaro Frosticos, and having mentioned my intention with all the vigour of fancy, he gravely considered my words, and after some awful meditations thus he spoke: '*Olough, ma genesat, istum fullanah, cum dera kargos belgarasah eseum balgo bartigos triangulissimus!* However', added he, 'it behoveth thee to consider and ponder well upon the perils and the multitudinous dangers in the way of that wight who thus advanceth in all the perambulation of adventures: and verily, most valiant sire and Baron, I hope thou wilt demean thyself with all that laudable gravity and precaution which, as is related in the three hundred and forty-seventh chapter of the Prophylactics, is of more consideration than all the merit in this terraqueous globe. Yes, most truly do I advise thee unto thy good, and speak unto thee, most valiant Munchausen, with the greatest esteem, and wish thee to succeed in thy voyage; for it is said, that in the interior realms of Africa there are tribes that can see but just three inches and a half beyond the extremity of their noses; and verily thou shouldest moderate thyself, even sure and slow; they stumble who walk fast. But we shall bring you unto the Lady Fragrantia, and have her opinion of the matter.' He then took from his pocket a cap of dignity, such as described in the most honourable and antique heraldry, and placing it upon my head, addressed me thus: 'As thou seemest again to revive the spirit of ancient adventure, permit me to place upon thy head this favour, as a mark of the esteem in which I hold thy valorous disposition.'

The Lady Fragrantia, my dear friends, was one of the most divine creatures in all Great Britain, and was desperately in love with me. She was drawing my portrait upon a piece of white satin, when the most noble Hilaro Frosticos advanced. He pointed to the cap of dignity which he had placed upon my head. 'I do declare, Hilaro,' said the lovely Fragrantia, ''tis pretty, 'tis interesting; I love you, and I like you, my dear Baron', said she, putting on another plume: 'this gives it an air more delicate and more fantastical. I do thus, my dear Munchausen, as your friend, yet you can reject or accept my present just as you please; but I like the fancy, 'tis a good one, and I mean to improve it: and against whatever enemies you go, I shall have the sweet satisfaction to remember you bear my favour on your head!'

I snatched it with trepidation, and gracefully dropping on my knees, I three times kissed it with all the rapture of romantic love. 'I swear,' cried I, 'by thy bright eyes, and by the lovely whiteness of thine arm, that no savage, tyrant, or enemy upon the face of the earth shall despoil me of this favour, while one drop of the blood of the Munchausens doth circulate in my veins! I will bear it triumphant through the realms of Africa, whither I now intend my course, and make it respected, even in the court of Prester John.'

'I admire your spirit,' replied she, 'and shall use my utmost interest at court to have you dispatched with every pomp, and as soon as possible; but here comes a most brilliant company indeed, Lady Carolina Wilhelmina Amelia Skeggs, Lord Spigot, and Lady Faucet, and the Countess of Belleair.'

After the ceremonies of introduction to this company were over, we proceeded to consult upon the business; and as the cause met with general applause, it was immediately determined that I should proceed without delay, as soon as I obtained the sovereign approbation. 'I am convinced,' said Lord Spigot, 'that if there be any thing really unknown and worthy of our most ardent curiosity, it must be in the immense regions of Africa; that country, which seems to be the oldest on the globe, and yet with the greater part of which we are almost utterly unacquainted; what prodigious wealth of gold and diamonds must not lie concealed in those torrid regions, when the very rivers on the coast pour forth continual specimens of golden sand! 'Tis my opinion, therefore, that the Baron deserves the applause of all Europe for his spirit, and merits the most powerful assistance of the sovereign.'

So flattering an approbation, you may be sure, was delightful to my heart, and with every confidence and joy I suffered them to take me to court that instant. After the usual ceremonies of introduction, suffice it to say that I met with every honour and applause that my most sanguine expectations could demand. I had always a taste for the fashionable *je ne sais quoi* of the most elegant society, and in the presence of all the sovereigns of Europe I ever found myself quite at home, and experienced from the whole court the most flattering esteem and admiration. I remember, one particular day, the fate of the unfortunate Marquis de Bellecourt. The Countess of Rassinda, who accompanied him, looked almost divinely. 'Yes, I am confident,' said the Marquis de Bellecourt to me, 'that I have acted according to the strictest sentiments of justice and of loyalty to my sovereign. What stronger breast-plate than a heart untainted? and though I did not receive a word nor a look, yet I cannot think—no, it were impossible to be misrepresented. Conscious of my own integrity, I will try again—I will go boldly up.' The Marquis de Bellecourt saw the opportunity; he advanced three paces, put his hand upon his breast and bowed. 'Permit me,' said he, 'with the most profound respect, to —— ' His tongue faltered—he could scarcely believe his sight, for at that moment the whole company were moving out of the room. He found himself almost alone, deserted by every one. 'What!' said he, 'and did he turn upon his heel with the most marked contempt? Would he not speak to me? Would he not ever hear me utter a word in my defence?' His heart died within him—not even a look, a smile from any one. 'My friends! Do they not know me? Do they not see me? Alas! they fear to catch the contagion of my —— Then,' said he, 'adieu!—'tis more than I can bear. I shall go to my country seat, and never, never will return. Adieu, fond court, adieu!—'

The venerable Marquis de Bellecourt stopped for a moment ere he entered his carriage. Thrice he looked back, and thrice he wiped the starting tear from his eye. 'Yes,' said he, 'for once, at least, truth shall be found—in the bottom of a well!'

Peace to thy ghost, most noble marquis! a King of kings shall pity thee; and thousands who are yet unborn shall owe their happiness to thee, and have cause to bless the thousands, perhaps, that shall never even know thy name; but Munchausen's self shall celebrate thy glory!

CHAPTER II

Preparations for the Baron's expedition into Africa—
Description of his chariot; the beauties of its interior
decorations; the animals that drew it, and the mechanism
of the wheels

Everything being concluded, and having received my in-
structions for the voyage, I was conducted by the illustrious Hilaro Frosticos, the Lady Fragrantia, and a prodigious
crowd of nobility, and placed sitting upon the summit of the
whale's bones at the palace; and having remained in this
situation for three days and three nights, as a trial ordeal, and
a specimen of my perseverance and resolution, the third hour
after midnight they seated me in the chariot of Queen Mab.
It was of a prodigious dimension, large enough to contain
more stowage than the tun of Heidelberg, and globular like
a hazel-nut; in fact, it seemed to be really a hazel-nut grown
to a most extravagant dimension, and that a great worm of
proportionable enormity had bored a hole in the shell.
Through this same entrance I was ushered. It was as large as a
coach-door, and I took my seat in the centre, a kind of chair
self-balanced without touching anything, like the fancied
tomb of Mahomet. The whole interior surface of the nutshell
appeared a luminous representation of all the stars of heaven,
the fixed stars, the planets, and a comet. The stars were as
large as those worn by our first nobility, and the comet,
excessively brilliant, seemed as if you had assembled all the
eyes of the beautiful girls in the kingdom, and combined
them, like a peacock's plumage, into the form of a comet—
that is, a globe, and a bearded tail to it, diminishing gradually

to a point. This beautiful constellation seemed very sportive and delightful. It was much in the form of a tadpole! and, without ceasing, went, full of playful giddiness, up and down, all over the heaven on the concave surface of the nutshell. One time it would be at that part of the heavens under my feet, and in the next minute would be over my head. It was never at rest, but for ever going east, west, north, or south, and paid no more respect to the different worlds than if they were so many lanterns without reflectors. Some of them he would dash against and push out of their places; others he would burn up and consume to ashes: and others again he would split into fritters, and their fragments would instantly take a globular form, like spilled quicksilver, and become satellites to whatever other worlds they should happen to meet with in their career. In short, the whole seemed an epitome of the creation, past, present, and future; and all that passes among the stars during one thousand years was here generally performed in as many seconds.

I surveyed all the beauties of the chariot with wonder and delight. 'Certainly,' cried I, 'this is heaven in miniature!' In short, I took the reins in my hand. But before I proceed on my adventures, I shall mention the rest of my attendant furniture. The chariot was drawn by a team of nine bulls harnessed to it, three after three. In the first rank was a most tremendous bull named John Mowmowsky; the rest were called Jacks in general, but not dignified by any particular denomination. They were all shod for the journey, not indeed like horses, with iron, or as bullocks commonly are, to drag on a cart; but were shod with men's skulls. Each of their feet was, hoof and all, crammed into a man's head, cut off for the purpose, and fastened therein with a kind of cement or paste, so that the skull seemed to be a part of the foot and hoof of the animal. With these skull-shoes the creatures could perform astonishing journeys, and slide upon the water, or upon the ocean, with great velocity. The harnesses were fastened with golden buckles, and decked with studs in a superb style, and the creatures were ridden by nine postilions, crickets of a great size, as large as monkeys, who sat squat upon the heads of the bulls, and were continually chirping at a most infernal rate, loud in proportion to their bodies.

The wheels of the chariot consisted of upwards of ten thousand springs, formed so as to give the greater impetuosity to the vehicle, and were more complex than a dozen clocks like that of Strasburgh. The external of the chariot was adorned with banners, and a superb festoon of laurel that formerly shaded me on horseback. And now, having given you a very concise description of my machine for travelling into Africa, which you must allow to be far superior to the apparatus of Monsieur Vaillant, I shall proceed to relate the exploits of my voyage.

CHAPTER III

The Baron proceeds on his voyage—Convoys a squadron to Gibraltar—Declines the acceptance of the island of Candia—His chariot damaged by Pompey's Pillar and Cleopatra's needle—The Baron out-does Alexander— Breaks his chariot, and splits a great rock at the Cape of Good Hope

Taking the reins in my hand, while the music gave a general salute, I cracked my whip, away they went, and in three hours I found myself just between the Isle of Wight and the main land of England. Here I remained four days, until I had received part of my accompaniment, which I was ordered to take under my convoy. 'Twas a squadron of men-of-war that had been a long time prepared for the Baltic, but which were now destined for the Mediterranean. By the assistance of large hooks and eyes, exactly such as are worn in our hats, but of a greater size, some hundredweight each, the men-of-war hooked themselves on to the wheels of the vehicle: and, in fact, nothing could be more simple or convenient, because they could be hooked or unhooked in an instant with the utmost facility. In short, having given a general discharge of their artillery, and three cheers, I cracked my whip, away we went, helter skelter, and in six jiffies I found myself and all my retinue safe and in good spirits just at the rock of Gibraltar. Here I unhooked my squadron, and having taken an affectionate leave of the officers, I suffered them to proceed in their ordinary manner to the place of their destination. The whole garrison were highly delighted with the novelty of my vehicle; and at the pressing solicitations of the governor and officers I went ashore, and took a view of that barren old rock, about which more powder has been fired away than would purchase twice as much fertile ground in any part of the world! Mounting my chariot, I took the reins, and again made forward, in mad career, down the Mediterranean to the isle of Candia. Here I received despatches from the Sublime Porte, entreating me to assist in the war against Russia, with a reward of the whole island of Candia for my alliance. At first I hesitated, thinking that the island of Candia would be a most valuable acquisition to the sovereign who at that time employed me, and that the most delicious wines, sugar, &c.,

in abundance would flourish on the island; yet, when I considered the trade of the East India Company, which would most probably suffer by the intercourse with Persia through the Mediterranean, I at once rejected the proposal, and had afterwards the thanks of the Honourable the House of Commons for my propriety and political discernment.

Having been properly refreshed at Candia, I again proceeded, and in a short time arrived in the land of Egypt. The land of this country, at least that part of it near the sea, is very low, so that I came upon it ere I was aware, and the pillar of Pompey got entangled in the various wheels of the machine, and damaged the whole considerably. Still I drove on through thick and thin, till, passing over that great obelisk, the Needle of Cleopatra, the work got entangled again, and jolted at a miserable rate over the mud and swampy ground of all that country; yet my poor bulls trotted on with astonishing labour across the Isthmus of Suez into the Red Sea, and left a track, an obscure channel, which has since been taken by De Tott for the remains of a canal cut by some of the Ptolemies from the Red Sea to the Mediterranean; but, as you perceive, was in reality no more than the track of my chariot, the car of Queen Mab.

As the artists at present in that country are nothing wonderful, though the ancient Egyptians, 'tis said, were most astonishing fellows, I could not procure any new coach-springs, or have a possibility of setting my machine to rights in the kingdom of Egypt; and as I could not presume to attempt another journey overland, and the great mountains of marble beyond the source of the Nile, I thought it most eligible to make the best way I could, by sea, to the Cape of Good Hope, where I supposed I should get some Dutch smiths and carpenters, or perhaps some English artists; and my vehicle being properly repaired, it was my intention thence to proceed, overland, through the heart of Africa. The surface of the water, I well knew, afforded less resistance to the wheels of the machine—it passed along the waves like the chariot of Neptune; and in short, having gotten upon the Red Sea, we scudded away to admiration through the pass of Babelmandeb to the great Western coast of Africa, where Alexander had not the courage to venture.

And really, my friends, if Alexander had ventured toward the Cape of Good Hope he most probably would have never returned. It is difficult to determine whether there were then any inhabitants in the more southern parts of Africa or not; yet, at any rate, this conqueror of the world would have made but a nonsensical adventure; his miserable ships, not contrived for a long voyage, would have become leaky, and foundered, before he could have doubled the Cape, and left his Majesty fairly beyond the limits of the then known world. Yet it would have been an august exit for an Alexander, after having subdued Persia and India, to be wandering the Lord knows where, to Jup or Ammon, perhaps, or on a voyage to the moon as an Indian chief once said to Captain Cook.

But, for my part, I was far more successful than Alexander; I drove on with the most amazing rapidity, and thinking to halt on shore at the Cape, I unfortunately drove too close, and shattered the right side wheels of my vehicle against the rock, now called the Table Mountain. The machine went against it with such impetuosity as completely shivered the rock in a horizontal direction; so that the summit of the mountain, in the form of a semi-sphere, was knocked into the sea, and the steep mountain becoming thereby flattened at the top, has since received the name of the Table Mountain, from its similarity to that piece of furniture.

Just as this part of the mountain was knocked off, the ghost of the Cape, that tremendous sprite which cuts such a figure in the Lusiad, was discovered sitting squat in an excavation formed for him in the centre of the mountain. He seemed just like a young bee in his little cell before he comes forth, or like a bean in a bean-pod; and when the upper part of the mountain was split across and knocked off, the superior half of his person was discovered. He appeared of a bottle-blue colour, and started, dazzled with the unexpected glare of the light: hearing the dreadful rattle of the wheels, and the loud chirping of the crickets, he was thunder-struck, and instantly giving a shriek, sunk down ten thousand fathoms into the earth, while the mountain, vomiting out some smoke, silently closed up, and left not a trace behind!

CHAPTER IV

The Baron secures his chariot, &c., at the Cape and takes his passage for England in a homeward-bound Indiaman— Wrecked upon an island of ice, near the coast of Guinea— Escapes from the wreck, and rears a variety of vegetables upon the island—Meets some vessels belonging to the negroes bringing white slaves from Europe, in retaliation, to work upon their plantations in a cold climate near the South Pole—Arrives in England, and lays an account of his expedition before the Privy Council—Great preparations for a new expedition—The Sphinx, Gog and Magog, and a great company attend him—The ideas of Hilaro Frosticos respecting the interior parts of Africa

I perceived with grief and consternation the miscarriage of all my apparatus; yet I was not absolutely dejected; a great mind is never known but in adversity. With permission to the Dutch governor the chariot was properly laid up in a great storehouse, erected at the water's edge, and the bulls received every refreshment possible after so terrible a voyage. Well, you may be sure they deserved it, and therefore every attendance was engaged for them, until I should return.

As it was not possible to do anything more I took my passage in a homeward-bound Indiaman, to return to London, and lay the matter before the Privy Council.

We met with nothing particular until we arrived upon the coast of Guinea, where, to our utter astonishment, we perceived a great hill, seemingly of glass, advancing against us in the open sea; the rays of the sun were reflected upon it with such splendour, that it was extremely difficult to gaze at the phenomenon. I immediately knew it to be an island of ice, and though in so very warm a latitude, determined to make all possible sail from such horrible danger. We did so, but all in vain, for about eleven o'clock at night, blowing a very hard gale, and exceedingly dark, we struck upon the island. Nothing could equal the distraction, the shrieks, and despair of the whole crew, until I, knowing there was not a moment to be lost, cheered up their spirits, and bade them not despond, but do as I should request them. In a few minutes the vessel was half full of water, and the enormous castle of ice that seemed to hem us in on every side, in some places falling in hideous fragments upon the deck, killed the one half of the crew; upon which, getting upon the summit of the mast, I contrived to make it fast to a great promontory of the ice, and calling to the remainder of the crew to follow me, we all escaped from the wreck, and got upon the summit of the island.

The rising sun soon gave us a dreadful prospect of our situation, and the loss, or rather icefication, of the vessel; for being closed in on every side with castles of ice during the night, she was absolutely frozen over and buried in such a manner that we could behold her under our feet, even in the central solidity of the island. Having debated what was best to be done, we immediately cut down through the ice, and got up some of the cables of the vessel, and the boats, which, making fast to the island, we towed it with all our might, determined to bring home island and all, or perish in the attempt. On the summit of the island we placed what oakum and dregs of every kind of matter we could get from the vessel, which, in the space of a very few hours, on account of the liquefying of the ice, and the warmth of the sun, were transformed into a very fine manure; and as I had some seeds of exotic vegetables in my pocket, we shortly had a sufficiency of fruits and roots growing upon the island to supply the whole crew, especially the bread-fruit tree, a few plants of which had been in the vessel; and another tree, which bore plum-puddings so very hot, and with such exquisite proportion of sugar, fruit, &c., that we all acknowledged it was not possible to taste anything of the kind more delicious in England: in short, though the scurvy had made such dreadful progress among the crew before our striking upon the ice, the supply of vegetables, and especially the bread-fruit and pudding-fruit, put an almost immediate stop to the distemper.

We had not proceeded thus many weeks, advancing with incredible fatigue by continual towing, when we fell in with a fleet of Negro-men, as they call them. These wretches, I must inform you, my dear friends, had found means to make prizes of those vessels from some Europeans upon the coast of Guinea, and tasting the sweets of luxury, had formed colonies in several new discovered islands near the south pole, where they had a variety of plantations of such matters as would only grow in the coldest climates. As the black inhabitants of Guinea were unsuited to the climate and excessive cold of the country, they formed the diabolical project of getting Christian slaves to work for them. For this purpose they sent vessels every year to the coast of Scotland, the northern parts of Ireland and Wales, and were even sometimes seen off the coast of Cornwall. And having purchased, or entrapped by fraud or violence, a great number of men, women, and children, they proceeded with their cargoes of human flesh to the other end of the world, and sold them to their planters, where they were flogged into obedience, and made to work like horses all the rest of their lives.

My blood ran cold at the idea, while every one on the island also expressed his horror that such an iniquitous traffic should be suffered to exist. But, except by open violence, it was found impossible to destroy the trade, on account of a barbarous prejudice, entertained of late by the negroes, that the white people have no souls! However, we were determined to attack them, and steering down our island upon them, soon overwhelmed them: we saved as many of the white people as possible, but pushed all the blacks into the water again. The poor creatures we saved from slavery were so overjoyed, that they wept aloud through gratitude, and we experienced every delightful sensation to think what happiness we should shower upon their parents, their brothers and sisters and children, by bringing them home safe, redeemed from slavery, to the bosom of their native country.

Having happily arrived in England, I immediately laid a statement of my voyage, &c., before the Privy Council, and entreated an immediate assistance to travel into Africa, and, if possible, refit my former machine, and take it along with the rest. Everything was instantly granted to my satisfaction, and I received orders to get myself ready for departure as soon as possible.

As the Emperor of China had sent a most curious animal as a present to Europe, which was kept in the Tower, and it being of an enormous stature, and capable of performing the voyage with *éclat*, she was ordered to attend me. She was called Sphinx, and was one of the most tremendous though magnificent figures I ever beheld. She was harnessed with superb trappings to a large flat-bottomed boat, in which was placed an edifice of wood, exactly resembling Westminster Hall. Two balloons were placed over it, tackled by a number of ropes to the boat, to keep up a proper equilibrium, and prevent it from overturning, or filling, from the prodigious weight of the fabric.

The interior of the edifice was decorated with seats, in the form of an amphitheatre, and crammed as full as it could hold with ladies and lords, as a council and retinue for your humble servant. Nearly in the centre was a seat elegantly decorated for myself, and on either side of me were placed the famous Gog and Magog in all their pomp.

The Lord Viscount Gosamer being our postilion, we floated gallantly down the river, the noble Sphinx gambolling like the huge leviathan, and towing after her the boat and balloons.

Thus we advanced, sailing gently, into the open sea; being calm weather, we could scarcely feel the motion of the vehicle, and passed our time in grand debate upon the glorious intention of our voyage, and the discoveries that would result.

'I am of opinion,' said my noble friend, Hilaro Frosticos, 'that Africa was originally inhabited for the greater part, or, I may say, subjugated by lions which, next to man, seem to be the most dreaded of all mortal tyrants. The country in general—at least, what we have been hitherto able to discover, seems rather inimical to human life; the intolerable dryness of the place, the burning sands that overwhelm whole armies and cities in general ruin, and the hideous life many roving hordes are compelled to lead, incline me to think, that if ever we form any great settlements therein, it will become the grave of our countrymen. Yet it is nearer to us than the East Indies, and I cannot but imagine, that in many places every production of China, and of the East and West Indies, would flourish, if properly attended to. And as the country is so prodigiously extensive and unknown, what a source of discovery must not it contain! In fact, we know less about the interior of Africa than we do of the moon; for in this latter we measure the very prominences, and observe the varieties and inequalities of the surface through our glasses,

Forests and mountains on her spotted orb.

'But we see nothing in the interior of Africa, but what some compilers of maps or geographers are fanciful enough to imagine. What a happy event, therefore, should we not expect from a voyage of discovery and colonization undertaken in so magnificent a style as the present! what a pride—what an acquisition to philosophy!'

CHAPTER V

Count Gosamer thrown by Sphinx into the snow on the top of Teneriffe—Gog and Magog conduct Sphinx for the rest of the voyage—The Baron arrives at the Cape, and unites his former chariot, &c., to his new retinue—Passes into Africa, proceeding from the Cape northwards— Defeats a host of lions by a curious stratagem—Travels through an immense desert—His whole company, chariot, &c., overwhelmed by a whirlwind of sand—Extricates them, and arrives in a fertile country

The brave Count Gosamer, with a pair of hell-fire spurs on, riding upon Sphinx, directed the whole retinue towards the Madeiras. But the Count had no small share of an amiable vanity, and perceiving great multitudes of people, Gascons, &c., assembled upon the French coast, he could not refrain from showing some singular capers, such as they had never seen before: but especially when he observed all the members of the National Assembly extend themselves along the shore, as a piece of French politeness, to honour this expedition, with Rousseau, Voltaire, and Beelzebub at their head; he set spurs to Sphinx, and at the same time cut and cracked away as hard as he could, holding in the reins with all his might, striving to make the creature plunge and show some uncommon diversion. But sulky and ill-tempered was Sphinx at the time: she plunged indeed—such a devil of a plunge, that she dashed him in one jerk over her head, and he fell precipitately into the water before her. It was in the Bay of Biscay, all the world knows a very boisterous sea, and Sphinx, fearing he would be drowned, never turned to the left or the right out of her way, but advancing furious, just stooped her head a little, and supped the poor count off the water, into her mouth, together with the quantity of two or three tuns of water, which she must have taken in along with him, but which were, to such an enormous creature as Sphinx, nothing more than a spoonful would be to any of you or me. She swallowed him, but when she had got him in her stomach, his long spurs so scratched and tickled her, that they produced the effect of an emetic. No sooner was he in, but out he was squirted with the most horrible impetuosity, like a ball or a shell from the calibre of a mortar. Sphinx was at this time quite sea-sick, and the unfortunate count was driven forth like a sky-rocket, and landed upon the peak of Teneriffe, plunged over head and ears in the snow—*requiescat in pace!*

I perceived all this mischief from my seat in the ark, but was in such a convulsion of laughter that I could not utter an intelligible word. And now Sphinx, deprived of her postilion, went on in a zigzag direction, and gambolled away after a most dreadful manner. And thus had everything gone to wreck, had I not given instant orders to Gog and Magog to sally forth. They plunged into the water, and swimming on each side, got at length right before the animal, and then seized the reins. Thus they continued swimming on each side, like tritons, holding the muzzle of Sphinx, while I, sallying forth astride upon the creature's back, steered forward on our voyage to the Cape of Good Hope.

Arriving at the Cape, I immediately gave orders to repair my former chariot and machines, which were very expeditiously performed by the excellent artists I had brought with me from Europe. And now everything being refitted, we launched forth upon the water: perhaps there never was anything seen more glorious or more august. 'Twas magnificent to behold Sphinx make her obeisance on the water, and the crickets chirp upon the bulls in return of the salute; while Gog and Magog advancing, took the reins of the great John Mowmowsky, and leading towards us chariot and all, instantly disposed of them to the forepart of the ark by hooks and eyes, and tackled Sphinx before all the bulls. Thus the whole had a most tremendous and triumphal appearance. In front floated forwards the mighty Sphinx, with Gog and Magog on each side; next followed in order the bulls with crickets upon their heads; and then advanced the chariot of Queen Mab, containing the curious seat and orrery of heaven; after which appeared the boat and ark of council, overtopped with two balloons, which gave an air of greater lightness and elegance to the whole. I placed in the galleries under the balloons, and on the backs of the bulls, a number of excellent vocal performers, with martial music of clarionets and trumpets. They sung the Watery Dangers, and the Pomp of Deep Cerulean! The sun shone glorious on the water while the procession advanced toward the land, under five hundred arches of ice, illuminated with coloured lights, and adorned in the most grotesque and fanciful style with sea-weed, elegant festoons, and shells of every kind; while a thousand waterspouts danced eternally before and after us, attracting the water from the sea in a kind of cone, and suddenly uniting with the most fantastical thunder and lightning.

Having landed our whole retinue, we immediately began to proceed toward the heart of Africa, but first thought it expedient to place a number of wheels under the ark for its greater facility of advancing. We journeyed nearly due north for several days, and met with nothing remarkable except the astonishment of the savage natives to behold our equipage.

The Dutch Government at the Cape, to do them justice, gave us every possible assistance for the expedition. I presume they had received instruction on that head from their High Mightinesses in Holland. However, they presented us with a specimen of some of the most excellent of their Cape wine, and shewed us every politeness in their power. As to the face of the country, as we advanced, it appeared in many places capable of every cultivation, and of abundant fertility. The natives and Hottentots of this part of Africa have been frequently described by travellers, and therefore it is not necessary to say any more about them. But in the more interior parts of Africa the appearance, manners, and genius of the people are totally different.

We directed our course by the compass and the stars, getting every day prodigious quantities of game in the woods, and at night encamping within a proper enclosure for fear of the wild beasts. One whole day in particular we heard on every side, among the hills, the horrible roaring of lions, resounding from rock to rock like broken thunder. It seemed as if there was a general rendezvous of all these savage animals to fall upon our party. That whole day we advanced with caution, our hunters scarcely venturing beyond pistol shot from the caravan for fear of dissolution. At night we encamped as usual, and threw up a circular entrenchment round our tents. We had scarce retired to repose when we found ourselves serenaded by at least one thousand lions, approaching equally on every side, and within a hundred paces. Our cattle showed the most horrible symptoms of fear, all trembling, and in cold perspiration. I directly ordered the whole company to stand to their arms, and not to make any noise by firing till I should command them. I then took a large quantity of tar, which I had brought with our caravan for that purpose, and strewed it in a continued stream round the encampment, within which circle of tar I immediately placed another train or circle of gunpowder, and having taken this precaution, I anxiously waited the lions' approach. These dreadful animals, knowing, I presume, the force of our troop, advanced very slowly, and with caution, approaching on every side of us with an equal pace, and growling in hideous concert, so as to resemble an earthquake, or some similar convulsion of the world. When they had at length advanced and steeped all their paws in the tar, they put their noses to it, smelling it as if it were blood, and daubed their great bushy hair and whiskers with it equal to their paws. At that very instant, when, in concert, they were to give the mortal dart upon us, I discharged a pistol at the train of gunpowder, which instantly exploded on every side, made all the lions recoil in general uproar, and take to flight with the utmost precipitation. In an instant we could behold them scattered through the woods at some distance, roaring in agony, and moving about like so many Will-o'-the-Wisps, their paws and faces all on fire from the tar and the gunpowder. I then ordered a general pursuit: we followed them on every side through the woods, their own light serving as our guide, until, before the rising of the sun, we followed into their fastnesses and shot or otherwise destroyed every one of them, and during the whole of our journey after we never heard the roaring of a lion, nor did any wild beast presume to make another attack upon our party, which shows the excellence of immediate presence of mind, and the terror inspired into the most savage enemies by a proper and well-timed proceeding.

We at length arrived on the confines of an immeasurable desert—an immense plain, extending on every side of us like an ocean. Not a tree, nor a shrub, nor a blade of grass was to be seen, but all appeared an extreme fine sand, mixed with gold-dust and little sparkling pearls.

The gold-dust and pearls appeared to us of little value, because we could have no expectation of returning to England for a considerable time. We observed, at a great distance, something like a smoke arising just over the verge of the horizon, and looking with our telescopes we perceived it to be a whirlwind tearing up the sand and tossing it about in the heavens with frightful impetuosity. I immediately ordered my company to erect a mound around us of a great size, which we did with astonishing labour and perseverance, and then roofed it over with certain planks and timber, which we had with us for the purpose. Our labour was scarcely finished when the sand came rolling in like the waves of the sea; 'twas a storm and river of sand united. It continued to advance in the same direction, without intermission, for three days, and completely covered over the mound we had erected, and buried us all within. The intense heat of the place was intolerable; but guessing, by the cessation of the noise, that the storm was passed, we set about digging a passage to the light of day again, which we effected in a very short time, and ascending, perceived that the whole had been so completely covered with the sand, that there appeared no hills, but one continued plain, with inequalities or ridges on it like the waves of the sea. We soon extricated our vehicle and retinue from the burning sands, but not without great danger, as the heat was very violent, and began to proceed on our voyage. Storms of sand of a similar nature several times attacked us, but by using the same precautions we preserved ourselves repeatedly from destruction. Having travelled more than nine thousand miles over this inhospitable plain, exposed to the perpendicular rays of a burning sun, without ever meeting a rivulet, or a shower from heaven to refresh us, we at length became almost desperate, when, to our inexpressible joy, we beheld some mountains at a great distance, and on our nearer approach observed them covered with a carpet of verdure and groves and woods. Nothing could appear more romantic or beautiful than the rocks and precipices intermingled with flowers and shrubs of every kind, and palm-trees of such a prodigious size as to surpass anything ever seen in Europe. Fruits of all kinds appeared growing wild in the utmost abundance, and antelopes and sheep and buffaloes wandered about the groves and valleys in profusion. The trees resounded with the melody of birds, and everything displayed a general scene of rural happiness and joy.

CHAPTER VI

*A feast on live bulls and kava—The inhabitants admire
the European adventurers—The Emperor comes to meet
the Baron, and pays him great compliments—The inhabitants of the centre of Africa descended from the people
of the moon proved by an inscription in Africa, and by
the analogy of their language, which is also the same with
that of the ancient Scythians—The Baron is declared
sovereign of the interior of Africa on the decease of the
Emperor—He endeavours to abolish the custom of eating
live bulls, which excites much discontent—The advice
of Hilaro Frosticos upon the occasion—The Baron makes
a speech to an Assembly of the states, which only excites
greater murmurs—He consults with Hilaro Frosticos*

Having passed over the nearest mountains we entered a
delightful vale where we perceived a multitude of
persons at a feast of living bulls, whose flesh they cut away
with great knives, making a table of the creature's carcase,
serenaded by the bellowing of the unfortunate animal. Nothing seemed requisite to add to the barbarity of this feast but
kava, made as described in Cook's voyages, and at the conclusion of the feast we perceived them brewing this liquor,
which they drank with the utmost avidity. From that moment, inspired with an idea of universal benevolence, I determined to abolish the custom of eating live flesh and drinking
of kava. But I knew that such a thing could not be immediately effected, whatever in future time might be performed.

Having rested ourselves during a few days, we determined
to set out towards the principal city of the empire. The singu-

larity of our appearance was spoken of all over the country as a phenomenon. The multitude looked upon Sphinx, the bulls, the crickets, the balloons, and the whole company, as something more than terrestrial, but especially the thunder of our fire-arms, which struck horror and amazement into the whole nation.

We at length arrived at the metropolis, situated on the banks of a noble river, and the emperor, attended by all his court, came out in grand procession to meet us. The emperor appeared mounted on a dromedary, royally caparisoned, with all his attendants on foot through respect for his Majesty. He was rather above the middle stature of that country, four feet three inches in height, with a countenance, like all his countrymen, as white as snow! He was preceded by a band of most exquisite music, according to the fashion of the country, and his whole retinue halted within about fifty paces of our troop. We returned the salute by a discharge of musketry, and a flourish of our trumpets and martial music. I commanded our caravan to halt, and dismounting, advanced uncovered, with only two attendants, towards his Majesty. The emperor was equally polite, and descending from his dromedary, advanced to meet me. 'I am happy,' said he, 'to have the honour to receive so illustrious a traveller, and assure you that everything in my empire shall be at your disposal.'

I thanked his Majesty for his politeness, and expressed how happy I was to meet so polished and refined a people in the centre of Africa, and that I hoped to show myself and company grateful for his esteem, by introducing the arts and sciences of Europe among the people.

I immediately perceived the true descent of this people, which does not appear of terrestrial origin, but descended from some of the inhabitants of the moon, because the principal language spoken there, and in the centre of Africa, is very nearly the same. Their alphabet and method of writing are pretty much the same, and show the extreme antiquity of this people, and their exalted origin. I here give you a specimen of their writing [*Vide Otrckocsus de Orig. Hung.* p. 46]—Sregnah, dna skoohtop.

These characters I have submitted to the inspection of a celebrated antiquarian, and it will be proved to the satisfaction of every one in his next volume, what an immediate intercourse there must have been between the inhabitants of the moon and the ancient Scythians, which Scythians did not by any means inhabit a part of Russia, but the central part of Africa, as I can abundantly prove to my very learned and laborious friend. The above words, written in our characters, are *Sregnah dna skoohtop;* that is, The Scythians are of heavenly origin. The word *Sregnah,* which signifies *Scythians,* is compounded of *sreg* or *sre,* whence our present English word sire, or sir: and *nah,* or *gnah,* knowledge, because the Scythians united the essentials of nobility and learning together: *dna* signifies heaven, or belonging to the moon, from *duna,* who was anciently worshipped as goddess of that luminary. And *skoohtop* signifies the origin or beginning of anything, from *skoo,* the name used in the moon for a point in geometry, and *top* or *toppas*, vegetation. These words are inscribed at this day upon a pyramid in the centre of Africa, nearly at the source of the river Niger; and if any one refuses his assent, he may go there to be convinced.

The emperor conducted me to his court amidst the admiration of his courtiers, and paid us every possible politeness that African magnificence could bestow. He never presumed to proceed on any expedition without consulting us, and looking upon us as a species of superior beings, paid the greatest respect to our opinions. He frequently asked me about the states of Europe, and the kingdom of Great Britain, and appeared lost in admiration at the account I gave him of our shipping, and the immensity of the ocean. We taught him to regulate the government nearly on the same plan with the British constitution, and to institute a parliament and degrees of nobility. His Majesty was the last of his royal line, and on his decease, with the unanimous consent of the people, made me heir to the whole empire. The nobility and chiefs of the country immediately waited upon me with petitions, entreating me to accept the government. I consulted with my noble friends, Gog and Magog, &c., and after much consultation it was agreed that I should accept the government, not as actual and independent monarch of the place, but as viceroy to his Majesty of England.

I now thought it high time to do away with the custom of eating of live flesh and drinking of kava, and for that purpose used every persuasive method to wean the majority of the people from it. This, to my astonishment, was not taken in good part by the nation, and they looked with jealousy at those strangers who wanted to make innovations among them.

Nevertheless, I felt much concern to think that my fellow-creatures could be capable of such barbarity. I did everything that a heart fraught with universal benevolence and good will to all mankind could be capable of desiring. I first tried every method of persuasion and incitement. I did not harshly reprove them, but I invited frequently whole thousands to dine, after the fashion of Europe, upon roasted meat. Alas, 'twas all in vain! my goodness nearly excited a sedition. They murmured among themselves, spoke of my intentions, my wild and ambitious views, as if I, O heaven! could have had any personal interested motive in making them live like men, rather than like crocodiles and tigers. In fine, perceiving that gentleness could be of no avail, well knowing that when complaisance can effect nothing from some spirits, compulsion excites respect and veneration, I prohibited, under the pain of the severest penalties, the drinking of kava, or eating of live flesh, for the space of nine days, within the districts of Anga-linar and Paphagalna.

But this created such a universal abhorrence and detestation of my government, that my ministers, and even myself, were universally pasquinadoed; lampoons, satires, ridicule, and insult, were showed upon the name of Munchausen wherever it was mentioned; and in fine, there never was a government so much detested, or with such little reason.

In this dilemma I had recourse to the advice of my noble friend Hilaro Frosticos. In his good sense I now expected some resource, for the rest of the council, who had advised me to the former method, had given but a poor specimen of their abilities and discernment, or I should have succeeded more happily. In short, he addressed himself to me and to the council as follows:

'It is in vain, most noble Munchausen, that your Excellency endeavours to compel or force these people to a life to which they have never been accustomed. In vain do you tell them that apple-pies, pudding, roast beef, minced pies, or tarts, are delicious, that sugar is sweet, that wine is exquisite. Alas! they cannot, they will not comprehend what deliciousness is, what sweetness, or what the flavour of the grape. And even if they were convinced of the superior excellence of your way of life, never, never would they be persuaded; and that if for no other reason, but because force or persuasion is employed to induce them to it. Abandon that idea for the present, and let us try another method. My opinion, therefore, is, that we should at once cease all endeavours to compel or persuade them. But let us, if possible, procure a quantity of *fudge* from England, and carelessly scatter it over all the country; and from this disposal of matters I presume—nay, I have a moral certainty, that we shall reclaim this people from horror and barbarity.'

Had this been proposed at any other time, it would have been violently opposed in the council; but now, when every other attempt had failed, when there seemed no other resource, the majority willingly submitted to they knew not what, for they absolutely had no idea of the manner, the possibility of success, or how they could bring matters to bear. However, 'twas a scheme, and as such they submitted. For my part, I listened with ecstasy to the words of Hilaro Frosticos, for I knew that he had a most singular knowledge of human kind, and could humour and persuade them on to their own happiness and universal good. Therefore, according to the advice of Hilaro, I despatched a balloon with four men over the desert to the Cape of Good Hope, with letters to be forwarded to England, requiring, without delay, a few cargoes of fudge.

The people had all this time remained in a general state of ferment and murmur. Everything that rancour, low wit, and deplorable ignorance could conceive to asperse my government, was put in execution. The most worthy, even the most beneficent actions, everything that was amiable, were perverted into opposition.

The heart of Munchausen was not made of such impenetrable stuff as to be insensible to the hatred of even the most worthless wretch in the whole kingdom; and once, at a general assembly of the states, filled with an idea of such continued ingratitude, I spoke as pathetic as possible, not, methought, beneath my dignity, to make them feel for me: that the universal good and happiness of the people were all I wished or desired; that if my actions had been mistaken, or improper surmises formed, still I had no wish, no desire, but the public welfare, &c. &c. &c.

Hilaro Frosticos was all this time much disturbed; he looked sternly at me—he frowned, but I was so engrossed with the warmth of my heart, my intentions, that I understood him not: in a minute I saw nothing but as if through a cloud (such is the force of amiable sensibility)—lords, ladies, chiefs—the whole assembly seemed to swim before my sight. The more I thought on my good intentions, the lampoons which so much affected my delicacy, good nature, tenderness—I forgot myself—I spoke rapid, violent—beneficence—fire—tenderness—alas! I melted into tears!

'Pish! pish!' said Hilaro Frosticos!

Now, indeed, was my government lampooned, satirized, carribonadoed, bepickled, and bedevilled. One day, with my arm full of lampoons, I started up as Hilaro entered the room, the tears in my eyes: 'Look, look here Hilaro!—how can I bear all this? It is impossible to please them; I will leave the government—I cannot bear it! See what pitiful anecdotes—what surmises: I will make my people feel for me—I will leave the government!'

'Pshaw!' says Hilaro. At that simple monosyllable I found myself changed as if by magic! for I ever looked on Hilaro as a person so experienced—such fortitude, such good sense. 'There are three sail, under the convoy of a frigate,' added Hilaro, 'just arrived at the Cape, after a fortunate passage, laden with the fudge that we demanded. No time is to be lost; let it be immediately conducted hither, and distributed through the principal granaries of the empire.'

CHAPTER VII

A proclamation by the Baron—Excessive curiosity of the people to know what fudge was—The people in a general ferment about it—They break open all the granaries in the empire—The affections of the people conciliated—An ode performed in honour of the Baron—His discourse with Fragrantia on the excellence of the music

Some time after I ordered the following proclamation to be published in the Court Gazette, and in all the other papers of the empire:

BY THE MOST MIGHTY AND PUISSANT LORD,

HIS EXCELLENCY THE

LORD BARON MUNCHAUSEN

WHEREAS a quantity of fudge has been distributed through all the granaries of the empire for particular uses; and as the natives have ever expressed their aversion to all manner of European eatables, it is hereby strictly forbidden, under pain of the severest penalties, for any of the officers charged with the keeping of the said fudge to give, sell, or suffer to be sold, any part or quantity whatever of the said material, until it be agreeable unto our good will and pleasure.

MUNCHAUSEN.

Dated in our Castle of Gristariska this
Triskill of the month of Griskish, in
the year Moulikasra-navas-kashna-
vildash.

This proclamation excited the most ardent curiosity all over the empire. 'Do you know what this fudge is?' said Lady Mooshilgarousti to Lord Darnarlaganl. 'Fudge!' said he, 'Fudge! no: what fudge?' 'I mean,' replied her Ladyship, 'the enormous quantity of fudge that has been distributed under guards in all the strong places in the empire, and which is strictly forbidden to be sold or given to any of the natives under the severest penalties.' 'Lord!' replied he, 'what in the name of wonder can it be? Forbidden! why it must, but pray do you, Lady Fashashash, do you know what this fudge is? Do you, Lord Trastillauex? or you, Miss Gristilarkash! What! nobody know what this fudge can be?'

It engrossed for several days the chit-chat of the whole empire. Fudge, fudge, fudge, resounded in all companies and in all places, from the rising until the setting of the sun; and even at night, when gentle sleep refreshed the rest of mortals, the ladies of all that country were dreaming of fudge!

'Upon my honour,' said Kitty, as she was adjusting her modesty piece before the glass, just after getting out of bed, 'there is scarce anything I would not give to know what this fudge can be.' 'La! my dear,' replied Miss Killnariska, 'I have been dreaming the whole night of nothing by fudge; I thought my lover kissed my hand, and pressed it to his bosom while I, frowning, endeavoured to wrest it from him: that he kneeled at my feet. No, never, never will I look at you, cried I, till you tell me what this fudge can be, or get me some of it. Begone! cried I, with all the dignity of offended beauty, majesty, and a tragic queen. Begone! never see me more, or bring me this delicious fudge. He swore, on the honour of a knight, that he would wander o'er the world, encounter every danger, perish in the attempt, or satisfy the angel of his soul.'

The chiefs and nobility of the nation, when they met together to drink their kava, spoke of nothing but fudge. Men, women, and children all, all talked of nothing but fudge. 'Twas a fury of curiosity, one general ferment, an universal fever—nothing but fudge could allay it.

But in one respect they all agreed, that government must have had some interested view in giving such positive orders to preserve it, and keep it from the natives of the country. Petitions were addressed to me from all quarters, from every corporation and body of men in the whole empire. The majority of the people instructed their constituents, and the parliament presented a petition, praying that I would be pleased to take the state of the nation under consideration, and give orders to satisfy the people, or the most dreadful consequences were to be apprehended. To these requests, at the entreaty of my council, I made no reply, or at best but unsatisfactory answers. Curiosity was on the rack; they forgot to lampoon the government, so engaged were they about the fudge. The great assembly of the states could think of nothing else. Instead of enacting laws for the regulation of the people, instead of consulting what should seem most wise, most excellent, they could think, talk, and harangue of nothing but fudge. In vain did the Speaker call to order; the more checks they got the more extravagant and inquisitive they were.

In short, the populace in many places rose in the most outrageous and tumultuous manner, forced open the granaries in all places in one day, and triumphantly distributed the fudge through the whole empire.

Whether on account of the longing, the great curiosity, imagination, or the disposition of the people, I cannot say—but they found it infinitely to their taste; 'twas an intoxication of joy, satisfaction, and applause.

Finding how much they liked this fudge, I procured another quantity from England, much greater than the former, and cautiously bestowed it over all the kingdom. Thus were the affections of the people regained; and they, from hence, began to venerate, applaud, and admire my government more than ever. The following ode was performed at the castle, in the most superb style, and universally admired:

ODE

Ye bulls and crickets, and Gog, Magog,
And trump'ts high chiming anthrophog,
Come sing blithe choral all in *og*,
Caralog, basilog, fog, and bog!

Great and superb appears thy cap sublime,
Admired and worshipp'd as the rising sun;
Solemn, majestic, wise, like hoary Time,
And fam'd alike for virtue, sense, and fun.

Then swell the noble strain with song,
    And elegance divine,
While goddesses around shall throng,
    And all the muses nine.

And bulls, and crickets, and Gog, Magog,
And trumpets chiming anthrophog,
Shall sing blithe choral all in *og*,
Caralog, basilog, fog, and bog!

This piece of poetry was much applauded, admired, and *encored* in every public assembly, celebrated as an astonishing effort of genius; and the music, composed by Minheer Gastrashbark Gkrghhbarwskhk, was thought equal to the sense!—Never was there anything so universally admired, the summit of the most exquisite wit, the keenest praise, the most excellent music.

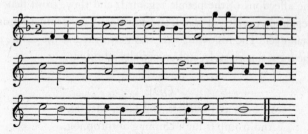

'Upon my honour, and the faith I owe my love,' said I, 'music may be talked of in England, but to possess the very soul of harmony the world should come to the performance of this ode.' Lady Fragrantia was at that moment drumming with her fingers on the edge of her fan, lost in a reverie, thinking she was playing upon—— Was it a forte piano?

'No, my dear Fragrantia,' said I, tenderly taking her in my

arms while she melted into tears; 'never, never, will I play upon any other——!'

Oh! 'twas divine, to see her like a summer's morning, all blushing and full of dew!

CHAPTER VIII

The Baron sets all the people of the empire to work to build a bridge from their country to Great Britain—His contrivance to render the arch secure—Orders an inscription to be engraved on the bridge—Returns with all his company, chariot, &c., to England—Surveys the kingdoms and nations under him from the middle of the bridge

'And now, most noble Baron,' said the illustrious Hilaro Frosticos, 'now is the time to make this people proceed in any business that we find convenient. Take them at this present ferment of the mind, let them not think, but at once set them to work.' In short, the whole nation went heartily to the business, to build an edifice such as was never seen in any other country. I took care to supply them with their favourite kava and fudge, and they worked like horses. The tower of Babylon, which, according to Hermogastricus, was seven miles high, or the Chinese wall, was a mere trifle, in comparison to this stupendous edifice, which was completed in a very short space of time.

It was of an immense height, far beyond anything that ever had been before erected, and of such gentle ascent, that a regiment of cavalry with a train of cannon could ascend with perfect ease and facility. It seemed like a rainbow in the heavens, the base of which appeared to rise in the centre of Africa, and the other extremity seemed to stoop into Great Britain. A most noble bridge indeed, and a piece of masonry that has outdone Sir Christopher Wren. Wonderful must it have been to form so tremendous an arch, especially as the artists had certain difficulties to labour against which they could not have in the formation of any other arch in the world —I mean, the attraction of the moon and planets: Because the arch was of so great a height, and in some parts so elongated from the earth, as in a great measure to diminish in its gravitation to the centre of our globe; or rather, seemed more easily operated upon by the attraction of the planets: So that the stones of the arch, one would think, at certain times, were ready to fall *up* to the moon, and at other times to fall down to the earth. But as the former was more to be dreaded, I secured stability to the fabric by a very curious contrivance: I ordered the architects to get the heads of some hundred numbskulls and blockheads, and fix them to the interior surface of the arch, at certain intervals, all the whole length, by which means the arch was held together firm, and its inclination to the earth eternally established; because of all the things in the world, the skulls of these kind of animals have a strange facility of tending to the centre of the earth.

The building being completed, I caused an inscription to be engraved in the most magnificent style upon the summit of the arch, in letters so great and luminous, that all vessels sailing to the East or West Indies might read them distinct in the heavens, like the motto of Constantine.

KARDOL BAGARLAN KAI TON FARINGO SARGAL RA MO PASHROL VATINEAC CAL COLNITOS RO NA FILNAT AGASTRA SA DINGANNAL FANO.

That is to say, 'As long as this arch and bond of union shall exist, so long shall the people be happy. Nor can all the power of the world affect them, unless the moon, advancing from her usual sphere, should so much attract the skulls as to cause a sudden elevation, on which the whole will fall into the most horrible confusion.'

An easy intercourse being thus established between Great Britain and the centre of Africa, numbers travelled continually to and from both countries, and at my request mail coaches were ordered to run on the bridge between both empires. After some time, having settled the government perfectly to my satisfaction, I requested permission to resign, as a great cabal had been excited against me in England; I therefore received my letters of recall, and prepared to return to Old England.

In fine, I set out upon my journey, covered with applause and general admiration. I proceeded with the same retinue that I had before—Sphinx, Gog and Magog, &c., and advanced along the bridge, lined on each side with rows of trees, adorned with festoons of various flowers, and illuminated with coloured lights. We advanced at a great rate along the bridge, which was so very extensive that we could scarcely perceive the ascent, but proceeded insensibly until we arrived on the centre of the arch. The view from thence was glorious beyond conception; 'twas divine to look down on the kingdoms and seas and islands under us. Africa seemed in general of a tawny brownish colour, burned up by the sun: Spain seemed more inclining to a yellow, on account of some fields of corn scattered over the kingdom; France appeared more inclining to a bright straw-colour, intermixed with green; and England appeared covered with the most beautiful verdure. I admired the appearance of the Baltic Sea, which evidently seemed to have been introduced between those countries by the sudden splitting of the land, and that originally Sweden was united to the western coast of Denmark; in short, the whole interstice of the Gulf of Finland had no being, until these countries, by mutual consent, separated from one another. Such were my philosophical meditations as I advanced, when I observed a man in armour, with a tremendous spear or lance, and mounted upon a steed, advancing against me. I soon discovered by a telescope that it could be no other than Don Quixote, and promised myself much amusement in the rencounter.

CHAPTER IX

The Baron's retinue is opposed in a heroic style by Don Quixote, who in his turn is attacked by Gog and Magog—Lord Whittington, with the Lord Mayor's show, comes to the assistance of Don Quixote—Gog and Magog assail his Lordship—Lord Whittington makes a speech, and deludes Gog and Magog to his party—A general scene of uproar and battle among the company, until the Baron, with great presence of mind, appeases the tumult

'What art thou?' exclaimed Don Quixote on his potent steed. 'Who art thou? Speak! or, by the eternal vengeance of mine arm, thy whole machinery shall perish at sound of this my trumpet!'

Astonished at so rude a salutation, the great Sphinx stopped short, and bridling up herself, drew in her head, like a snail when it touches something that it does not like: the bulls set up a horrid bellowing, the crickets sounded an alarm, and Gog and Magog advanced before the rest. One of these powerful brothers had in his hand a great pole, to the extremity of which was fastened a cord of about two feet in length, and to the end of the cord was fastened a ball of iron, with spikes shooting from it like the rays of a star; with this weapon he prepared to encounter, and advancing thus he spoke:

'Audacious wight! that thus, in complete steel arrayed, doth dare to venture cross my way, to stop the great Munchausen. Know then, proud knight, that thou shalt instant perish 'neath my potent arm.'

When Quixote, Mancha's knight, responded firm:

'Gigantic monster! leader of witches, crickets, and chimeras dire! know thou, that here before yon azure heaven the cause of truth, of valour, and of faith right pure shall ordeal counter try it!'

Thus he spoke, and brandishing his mighty spear, would instant prodigies sublime performed, had not some wight placed 'neath the tail of dark Rosinante furze all thorny base; at which, quadrupedanting, plunged the steed, and instant on the earth the knight roared *credo* for his life.

At that same moment ten thousand frogs started from the morions of Gog and Magog, and furiously assailed the knight on every side. In vain he roared, and invoked fair Dulcinea del Toboso: for frogs' wild croaking seemed more loud, more sonorous than all his invocations. And thus in battle vile the knight was overcome, and spawn all swarmed upon his glittering helmet.

'Detested miscreants!' roared the knight; 'avaunt! Enchant-

ers dire and goblins could alone this arduous task perform; to
rout the knight of Mancha, foul defeat, and war, even such as
ne'er was known before. Then hear, O del Toboso! hear my
vows, that thus in anguish of my soul I urge, 'midst frogs,
Gridalbin, Hecaton, Kai, Talon, and the Rove! [for such the
names and definitions of their qualities, their separate powers.]
For Merlin plumed their airy flight, and then in watery moon-
beam dyed his rod eccentric. At the touch ten thousand frogs,
strange metamorphosed, croaked even thus: And here they
come, on high behest, to vilify the knight that erst defended
famed virginity, and matrons all bewronged, and pilgrims
hoar, and courteous guise of all! But the age of chivalry is
gone, and the glory of Europe is extinguished for ever!'

He spake, and sudden good Lord Whittington, at head of
all his raree-show, came forth, armour antique of chivalry,

and helmets old, and troops, all streamers, flags and banners glittering gay, red, gold, and purple; and in every hand a square of gingerbread, all gilded nice, was brandished awful. At a word, ten thousand thousand Naples biscuits, crackers, buns, and flannel-cakes, and hats of gingerbread encountered in mid air in glorious exaltation, like some huge storm of mill-stones, or when it rains whole clouds of dogs and cats.

The frogs, astonished, thunderstruck, forgot their notes and music, that before had seemed so terrible, and drowned the cries of knight renown, and mute in wonder heard the words of Whittington, pronouncing solemn: 'Goblins, chimeras dire, or frogs, or whatsoe'er enchantment thus presents in antique shape, attend and hear the words of peace; and thou, good herald, read aloud the Riot Act!'

He ceased, and dismal was the tone that softly breathed from all the frogs in chorus, who quick had petrified with fright, unless redoubted Gog and Magog, both with poles, high topped with airy bladders by a string dependent, had not stormed against his lordship. Ever and anon the bladders, loud resounding on his chaps, proclaimed their fury against all potent law, coercive mayoralty; when he, submissive, thus in cunning guile addressed the knights assailant: 'Gog, Magog, renowned and famous! what, my sons, shall you assail your father, friend, and chief confessed? Shall you, thus armed with bladders vile, attack my title, eminence, and pomp sublime? Subside, vile discord, and again return to your true 'legiance. Think, my friends, how oft your gorgeous pouch I've crammed, all calapash, green fat, and calapee. Remember how you've feasted, stood inert for ages, until size immense you've gained. And think, how different is the service of Munchausen, where you o'er seas, cold, briny, float along the tide, eternal toiling like to slaves Algiers and Tripoli. And ev'n on high, balloon like, through the heavens have journeyed late, upon a rainbow or some awful bridge stretched eminent, as if on earth he had not work sufficient to distress your potent servitudes, but he should also seek in heaven dire cause of labour! Recollect, my friends, even why or wherefore should you thus assail your lawful magistrate, or why desert his livery? or for what or wherefore serve this German Lord Munchausen, who for all your labour shall alone bestow some fudge and heroic blows in war? Then cease, and thus in amity return to friendship aldermanic, bungy, brown, and sober.'

Ceased he then, right worshipful, when both the warring champions instant stemmed their battle, and in sign of peace and unity returning, 'neath their feet reclined their weapons. Sudden at a signal either stamped his foot sinistrine, and the loud report of bursten bladder stunned each ear surrounding, like the roar of thunder from on high convulsing heaven and earth.

'Twas now upon the saddle once again the knight of Mancha rose, and in his hand far balancing his lance, full tilt against the troops of bulls opposing ran. And thou, shrill Crillitrilkril, than whom no cricket e'er on hob of rural cottage, or chimney black, more gladsome tuned his merry note, e'en thou didst perish, shrieking gave the ghost in empty air, the sport of every wind; for e'en that heart so jocund and so gay was pierced, harsh spitted by the lance of Mancha, while undaunted thou didst sit between the horns that crowned Mowmowsky. And now Whittington advanced, 'midst armour antique and the powers Magog and Gog, and with his rod enchanting touched the head of every frog, long mute and thunderstruck, at which, in universal chorus and salute, they sung blithe jocund, and amain advance rebellious 'gainst my troop.

While Sphinx, though great, gigantic, seemed instinctive base and cowardly, and at the sight of storming gingerbread, and powers, Magog and Gog, and Quixote, all against her, started fierce, o'erturning boat, balloons, and all; loud roared the bulls, hideous, and the crash of wheels, and chaos of confusion drear, resounded far from earth to heaven. And still more fierce in charge the great Lord Whittington, from poke of ermine his famed Grimalkin took. She screamed, and harsh attacked my bulls confounded; lightning-like she darted, and from half the troop their eyes devouring tore. Nor could the riders, crickets throned sublime, escape from rage, from fury less averse, than cannons murder o'er the stormy sea. The great Mowmowsky roared amain and plunged in anguish, shunning every dart of fire-eyed fierce Grimalkin. Dire the rage of warfare and contending crickets, Quixote and great Magog; when Whittington advancing—'Good, my friends and warriors, headlong on the foe bear down impetuous.' He spoke, and waving high the mighty rod, tipped wonderful each bull, at which more fierce the creatures bellowed, while enchantment drear devoured their vitals. And all had gone to wreck in more than mortal strife, unless, like Neptune orient from the stormy deep, I rose, e'en towering o'er the ruins of my fighting troops. Serene and calm I stood, and gazed around undaunted; nor did aught oppose against my foes impetuous. But sudden from chariot purses plentiful of fudge poured forth, and scattered it amain o'er all the crowd contending. As when old Catherine or the careful Joan doth scatter to the chickens bits of bread and crumbs fragmented, while rejoiced they gobble fast the proffered scraps in general plenty and fraternal peace, and 'hush', she cries, 'hush! hush!'

CHAPTER X

*The Baron arrives in England—The Colossus of Rhodes
comes to congratulate him—Great rejoicings on the
Baron's return, and a tremendous concert—The Baron's
discourse with Fragrantia, and her opinion of the Tour to
the Hebrides*

Having arrived in England once more the greatest rejoicings were made for my return; the whole city seemed
one general blaze of illumination, and the Colossus of Rhodes,
hearing of my astonishing feats, came on purpose to England
to congratulate me on such unparalleled achievements. But
above all other rejoicings on my return, the musical oratorio
and song of triumph were magnificent in the extreme. Gog
and Magog were ordered to take the maiden tower of Windsor, and make a tambourine or great drum of it. For this
purpose they extended an elephant's hide, tanned and prepared for the design, across the summit of the tower, from
parapet to parapet, so that in proportion this extended elephant's hide was to the whole of the castle what the parchment
is to a drum, in such a manner that the whole became one
great instrument of war.

To correspond with this, Colossus took Guildhall and
Westminster Abbey, and turning the foundations towards
the heavens, so that the roofs of the edifices were upon the
ground, he strung them across with brass and steel wire from
side to side, and thus, when strung, they had the appearance of
most noble dulcimers. He then took the great dome of St
Paul's, raising it off the earth with as much facility as you
would a decanter of claret. And when once risen up it had the

appearance of a quart bottle. Colossus instantly, with his teeth, cracked off the superior part of the cupola, and then applying his lips to the instrument, began to sound it like a trumpet. 'Twas martial, beyond description—*tantara!*—*tara—ta!*

During the concert I walked in the park with Lady Fragrantia: she was dressed that morning in a *chemise à la reine*. 'I like,' said she, 'the dew of the morning, 'tis delicate and ethereal, and, by thus bespangling me, I think it will more approximate me to the nature of the rose (for her looks were like Aurora); and to confirm the vermilion I shall go to Spa.' 'And drink the Pouhon spring,' added I, gazing at her from top to toe. 'Yes,' replied the lovely Fragrantia, 'with all my heart; 'tis the drink of sweetness and delicacy. Never were there any creatures like the water-drinkers at Spa; they seem like so many thirsty blossoms on a peach-tree, that suck up the shower in the scorching heat. There is a certain something in the waters that gives vigour to the whole frame, and expands every heart with rapture and benevolence. They drink! good gods! how they do drink! and then, how they —! Pray my dear Baron, were you ever at the falls of Niagara?' 'Yes, my lady,' replied I, surprised at such a strange association of ideas; 'I have been, many years ago, at the Falls of Niagara, and found no more difficulty in swimming up and down the cataracts than I should to move a minuet.' At that moment she dropped her nosegay. 'Ah,' said she, as I presented it to her, 'there is no great variety in these polyanthuses. I do assure you, my dear Baron, that there is taste in the selection of flowers as well as everything else, and were I a girl of sixteen I should wear some rose-buds in my bosom, but at five-and-twenty think it would be more *apropos* to wear a full-blown rose, quite ripe, and ready to drop off the stalk for want of being pulled—heigh-ho!' 'But pray, my lady,' said I, 'how do you like the concert?' 'Alas!' said she, languishingly, while she laid her hand upon my shoulder 'what are these bodiless sounds and vibration to me? and yet what an exquisite sweetness in the songs of the northern part of our island: "*Thou art gone awa' from me, Mary!*" How pathetic and divine the little airs of Scotland and the Hebrides! But never, never can I think of that same Doctor Johnson—that CONSTABLE, as Fergus MacLeod calls him—but I have an idea of a great brown full-bottomed wig and a hogshead of porter! Oh, 'twas base! to be treated everywhere with politeness and hospitality, and in return invidiously to smellfungus them all over; to go to the country of Kate of Aberdeen, of Auld Robin Gray, 'midst rural innocence and sweetness, take up their plaids, and dance. Oh! Doctor, Doctor!'

'And what would you say, Fragrantia, if you were to write a tour to the Hebrides?' 'Peace to the heroes,' replied she, in a delicate and theatrical tone; 'peace to the heroes who sleep in the isle of Iona; the sons of the wave, and the chiefs of the dark-brown shield! The tear of the sympathizing stranger is scattered by the wind over the hoary stones as she meditates sorrowfully on the times of old! Such could I say, sitting upon some druidical heap or tumulus. The fact is this, there is a right and wrong handle to everything, and there is more pleasure in thinking with pure nobility of heart, than with the illiberal enmities and sarcasm of a blackguard.'

CHAPTER XI

A litigated contention between Don Quixote, Gog, Magog, &c.—A grand court assembled upon it—The appearance of the company—The matrons, judges, &c.— The method of writing, and the use of the fashionable amusement quizzes—Wauwau arrives from the country of Prester John, and leads the whole Assembly a wildgoose chase to the top of Plinlimmon, and thence to Virginia— The Baron meets a floating island in his voyage to America —Pursues Wauwau with his whole company through the deserts of North America—His curious contrivance to seize Wauwau in a morass

The contention between Gog and Magog, and Sphinx, Hilaro Frosticos, the Lord Whittington, &c., was productive of infinite litigation. All the lawyers in the kingdom were employed, to render the affair as complex and gloriously uncertain as possible; and, in fine, the whole nation became interested, and were divided on both sides of the question. Colossus took the part of Sphinx, and the affair was at length submitted to the decision of a grand council in a great hall, adorned with seats on every side in form of an amphitheatre. The assembly appeared the most magnificent and splendid in the world. A court or jury of one hundred matrons occupied the principal and most honourable part of the amphitheatre; they were dressed in flowing robes of sky-blue velvet adorned with festoons of brilliants and diamond stars; grave and sedate looking matrons, all in uniform, with spectacles upon their noses; and opposite to these were placed one hundred judges, with curly white wigs flowing down on each side of them to their very feet, so that Solomon in all his glory was not so wise in appearance. At the ardent request of the whole empire I condescended to be the president of the court, and being arrayed accordingly, I took my seat beneath a canopy erected in the centre. Before every judge was placed a square inkstand, containing a gallon of ink, and pens of a proportionable size; and also right before him an enormous folio, so large as to serve for table and book at the same time. But they did not make much use of their pens and ink, except to blot and daub the paper; for, that they should be the more impartial, I had ordered that none but the blind should be honoured with the employment: so that when they attempted to write anything, they uniformly dipped their pens into the machine containing sand, and having scrawled over a page as they thought, desiring them to dry it with sand, would spill half a gallon of ink upon the paper, and thereby daubing their fingers, would transfer the ink to their face whenever they leaned their cheek upon their hand for greater gravity. As to the matrons, to prevent an eternal prattle that would drown all manner of intelligibility, I found it absolutely necessary to sew up their mouths; so that between the blind judges and the dumb matrons methought the trial had a chance of being terminated sooner than it otherwise would. The matrons, instead of their tongues, had other instruments to convey their ideas: each of them had three quizzes, one quiz pendant from the string that sewed up her mouth, and another quiz in either hand. When she wished to express her negative, she darted and recoiled the quizzes in her right and left hand; and when she desired to express her affirmative, she, nodding, made the quiz pendant from her mouth flow down and recoil again. The trial proceeded in this manner for a long time, to the admiration of the whole empire, when at length I thought proper to send to my old friend and ally, Prester John, entreating him to forward to me one of the species of wild and curious birds found in his kingdom, called a Wauwau. This creature was brought over the great bridge, before mentioned, from the interior of Africa, by a balloon. The balloon was placed upon the bridge, extending over the parapets on each side, with great wings or oars to assist its velocity, and under the balloon was placed pendant a kind of boat, in which were the persons to manage the steerage of the machine, and protect Wauwau. This oracular bird, arriving in England, instantly darted through one of the windows of the great hall, and perched upon the canopy in the centre, to the admiration of all present. Her cackling appeared quite prophetic and oracular; and the first question proposed to her by the unanimous consent of the matrons and judges was, Whether or not the moon was composed of green cheese? The solution of this question was deemed absolutely necessary before they could proceed farther on the trial.

Wauwau seemed in figure not very much differing from a swan, except that the neck was not near so long, and she stood after an admirable fashion like to Vestris. She began cackling most sonorously, and the whole assembly agreed that it was absolutely necessary to catch her, and having her in their immediate possession, nothing more would be requisite for the termination of this litigated affair. For this purpose the whole house rose up to catch her, and approached in tumult, the judges brandishing their pens, and shaking their big wigs, and the matrons quizzing as much as possible in every direction, which very much startled Wauwau, who, clapping her wings, instantly flew out of the hall. The assembly began to proceed after her in order and style of precedence, together with my whole train of Gog and Magog, Sphinx, Hilaro Frosticos, Queen Mab's chariot, the bulls and crickets, &c., preceded by bands of music; while Wauwau, descending on the earth, ran on like an ostrich before the troop, cackling all the way. Thinking suddenly to catch this ferocious animal, the judges and matrons would suddenly quicken their pace, but the creature would as quickly outrun them, or sometimes fly away for many miles together, and then alight to take breath until we came within sight of her again. Our train journeyed over a most prodigious tract of country in a direct line, over hills and dales, to the summit of Plinlimmon, where we thought to have seized Wauwau; but she instantly took flight, and never ceased until she arrived at the mouth of the Potomac river in Virginia.

Our company immediately embarked in the machines before described, in which we had journeyed into Africa, and after a few days' sail arrived in North America. We met with nothing curious on our voyage, except a floating island, containing some very delightful villages, inhabited by a few whites and negroes; the sugar cane did not thrive there well, on account, as I was informed, of the variety of the climates; the island being sometimes driven up as far as the north pole, and at other times wafted under the equinoctial. In pity to the poor islanders, I got a huge stake of iron, and driving it through the centre of the island, fastened it to the rocks and mud at the bottom of the sea, since which time the island has become stationary, and is well known at present by the name of St Christopher's, and there is not an island in the world more secure.

Arriving in North America, we were received by the President of the United States with every honour and politeness. He was pleased to give us all the information possible relative to the woods and immense regions of America, and ordered troops of the different tribes of the Esquimaux to guide us through the forests in pursuit of Wauwau, who, we at length found, had taken refuge in the centre of a morass. The inhabitants of the country, who loved hunting, were much delighted to behold the manner in which we attempted to seize upon Wauwau; the chase was noble and uncommon. I determined to surround the animal on every side, and for this purpose ordered the judges and matrons to surround the morass with nets extending a mile in height, on various parts of which net the company disposed themselves, floating in the air like so many spiders upon their cobwebs. Magog, at my command, put on a kind of armour that he had carried with him for the purpose, corslet of steel, with gauntlets, helmet, &c., so as nearly to resemble a mole. He instantly plunged into the earth, making way with his sharp steel head-piece, and tearing up the ground with his iron claws, and found not much difficulty therein, as morass in general is of a soft and yielding texture. Thus he hoped to undermine Wauwau, and suddenly rising, seize her by the foot, while his brother Gog ascended the air in a balloon, hoping to catch her if she should escape Magog. Thus the animal was surrounded on every side, and at first was very much terrified, knowing not which way she had best to go. At length hearing an obscure noise under ground, Wauwau took flight before Magog could have time to catch her by the foot. She flew to the right, then to the left, north, east, west, and south, but found on every side the company prepared upon their nets. At length she flew right up, soaring at a most astonishing rate towards the sun, while the company on every side set up one general acclamation. But Gog in his balloon soon stopped Wauwau in the midst of her career, and snared her in a net, the cords of which he continued to hold in his hand. Wauwau did not totally lose her presence of mind, but, after a little consideration, made several violent darts against the volume of the balloon; so fierce, as at length to tear open a great space, on which the inflammable air rushing out, the whole apparatus began to tumble to the earth with amazing rapidity. Gog himself was thrown out of the vehicle, and letting go the reins of the net, Wauwau got liberty again, and flew out of sight in an instant.

Gog had been above a mile elevated from the earth when he began to fall, and as he advanced the rapidity increased, so that he went like a ball from a cannon into the morass, and his nose striking against one of the iron-capped hands of his brother Magog, just then rising from the depths, he began to bleed violently, and, but for the softness of the morass, would have lost his life.

CHAPTER XII

*The Baron harangues the company, and they continue the
pursuit—The Baron, wandering from his retinue, is taken
by the savages, scalped, and tied to a stake to be roasted;
but he contrives to extricate himself, and kills the savages
—The Baron travels overland through the forests of
North America, to the confines of Russia—Arrives at the
castle of the Nareskin Rowskimowmowsky, and gallops
into the kingdom of Loggerheads—A battle, in which the
Baron fights the Nareskin in single combat, and generously
gives him his life—Arrives at the Friendly Islands, and
discourses with Omai—The Baron, with all his attendants, goes from Otaheite to the isthmus of Darien, and
having cut a canal across the isthmus, returns to England*

'My friends, and very learned and profound Judiciarii,'
said I, 'be not disheartened that Wauwau has escaped
from you at present: persevere, and we shall still succeed. You
should never despair, Munchausen being your general; and
therefore be brave, be courageous, and fortune shall second
your endeavours. Let us advance undaunted in pursuit, and
follow the fierce Wauwau even three times round the globe,
until we entrap her.'

My words filled them with confidence and valour, and they
unanimously agreed to continue the chase. We penetrated the
frightful deserts and gloomy woods of America, beyond the
source of the Ohio, through countries utterly unknown
before. I frequently took the diversion of shooting in the
woods, and one day that I happened with three attendants to
wander far from our troop, we were suddenly set upon by a

number of savages. As we had expended our powder and shot, and happened to have no side arms, it was in vain to make any resistance against hundreds of enemies. In short, they bound us, and made us walk before them to a gloomy cavern in a rock, where they feasted upon what game they had killed, but which not being sufficient, they took my three unfortunate companions and myself, and scalped us. The pain of losing the flesh from my head was most horrible; it made me leap in agonies, and roar like a bull. They then tied us to stakes, and making great fires around us, began to dance in a circle, singing with much distortion and barbarity, and at times putting the palms of their hands to their mouths, set up the war-whoop. As they had on that day also made a great prize of some wine and spirits belonging to our troop, these bar-barians, finding it delicious, and unconscious of its intoxicat-ing quality, began to drink it in profusion, while they beheld us roasting, and in a very short time they were all completely drunk, and fell asleep around the fires. Perceiving some hopes, I used most astonishing efforts to extricate myself from the cords with which I was tied, and at length succeeded. I imme-diately unbound my companions, and though half roasted, they still had power enough to walk. We sought about for the flesh that had been taken off our heads, and having found the scalps, we immediately adapted them to our bloody heads, sticking them on with a kind of glue of a sovereign quality, that flows from a tree in that country, and the parts united and healed in a few hours. We took care to revenge ourselves on the savages, and with their own hatchets put every one of them to death. We then returned to our troop, who had given us up for lost, and they made great rejoicings on our return. We now proceeded in our journey through this prodigious wilderness, Gog and Magog acting as pioneers, hewing down the trees, &c., at a great rate as we advanced. We passed over numberless swamps and lakes and rivers, until at length we discovered a habitation at some distance. It appeared a dark and gloomy castle, surrounded with strong ramparts, and a broad ditch. We called a council of war, and it was determined to send a deputation with a trumpet to the walls of the castle, and demand friendship from the governor, whoever he might be, and an account if aught he knew of Wauwau. For this purpose our whole caravan halted in the wood, and Gog and Magog reclined amongst the trees, that their enormous strength and size should not be discovered, and give umbrage to the lord of the castle. Our embassy approached the castle, and having demanded admittance for some time, at length the drawbridge was let down, and they were suffered to enter. As soon as they had passed the gate it was immediately closed after them, and on either side they perceived ranks of halberdiers, who made them tremble with fear. 'We come,' the herald proclaimed, 'on the part of Hilaro Frosticos, Don Quixote, Lord Whittington, and the thrice-renowned Baron Munchausen, to claim friendship from the governor of this puissant castle, and to seek Wauwau.' 'The most noble the governor,' replied an officer, 'is at all times happy to entertain such travellers as pass through these immense deserts, and will esteem it an honour that the great Hilaro Frosticos, Don Quixote, Lord Whittington, and the thrice-renowned Baron Munchausen, enter his castle walls.'

In short, we entered the castle. The governor sat with all our company to table, surrounded by his friends, of a very fierce and warlike appearance. They spoke but little, and seemed very austere and reserved, until the first course was served up. The dishes were brought in by a number of bears walking on their hind-legs, and on every dish was a fricassee of pistols, pistol-bullets, sauce of gun-powder, and aqua-vitæ. This entertainment seemed rather indigestible by even an ostrich's stomach, when the governor addressed us, and informed me that it was ever his custom to strangers to offer them for the first course a service similar to that before us: and if they were inclined to accept the invitation, he would fight them as much as they pleased, but if they could not relish the pistol-bullets, &c., he would conclude them peaceable, and try what better politeness he could show them in his castle. In short, the first course being removed untouched, we dined, and after dinner the governor forced the company to push the bottle about with alacrity and to excess. He informed us that he was the Nareskin Rowskimowmowsky, who had retired amidst these wilds, disgusted with the court of Petersburgh. I was rejoiced to meet him; I recollected my old friend, whom I had known at the court of Russia, when I rejected the hand of the Empress. The Nareskin, with all his knights-companions, drank to an astonishing degree, and we all set off upon hobby horses in full cry out of the castle. Never was there seen such a cavalcade before. In front galloped a hundred knights belonging to the castle, with hunting horns and a pack of excellent dogs; and then came the Nareskin Rowskimowmowsky, Gog and Magog, Hilaro Frosticos, and your humble servant, hallooing and shouting like so many demoniacs, and spurring our hobby horses at an infernal rate until we arrived in the kingdom of Loggerheads. The kingdom of Loggerheads was wilder than any part of Siberia, and the Nareskin had here built a romantic summer-house in a Gothic taste, to which he would frequently retire with his company after dinner. The Nareskin had a dozen bears of enormous stature that danced for our amusement, and their chiefs performed the *minuet de la cour* to admiration. And here the most noble Hilaro Frosticos thought proper to ask the Nareskin some intelligence about Wauwau, in quest of whom we had travelled over such a tract of country, and encountered so many dangerous adventures, and also invited the Nareskin Rowskimowmowsky to attend us with all his bears in the expedition. The Nareskin appeared astonished at the idea; he looked with infinite hauteur and ferocity on Hilaro, and affecting a violent passion, asked him, Did he imagine that the Nareskin Rowskimowmowsky could condescend to take notice of a Wauwau, let her fly what way she would? Or did he think a chief possessing such blood in his veins could engage in such a foreign pursuit? By the blood of all the bears in the kingdom of Loggerheads, and by the ashes of my great great grandmother, I would cut off your head!

Hilaro Frosticos resented this oration, and in short a general riot commenced. The bears, together with the hundred knights, took the part of the Nareskin, and Gog and Magog Don Quixote, the Sphinx, Lord Whittington, the bulls, the crickets, the judges, the matrons, and Hilaro Frosticos, made noble warfare against them.

I drew my sword, and challenged the Nareskin to single combat. He frowned, while his eyes sparkled fire and indignation, and bracing a buckler on his left arm, he advanced against me. I made a blow at him with all my force, which he received upon his buckler, and my sword broke short.

Ungenerous Nareskin! seeing me disarmed, he still pushed forward, dealing his blows upon me with the utmost violence, which I parried with my shield and the hilt of my broken sword, and fought like a game-cock.

An enormous bear at the same time attacked me, but I ran my hand still retaining the hilt of my broken sword down his throat, and tore up his tongue by the roots. I then seized his carcase by the hind-legs, and whirling it over my head, gave the Nareskin such a blow with his own bear as evidently stunned him. I repeated my blows, knocking the bear's head against the Nareskin's head, until, by one happy blow, I got his head into the bear's jaws, and the creature being still somewhat alive and convulsive, the teeth closed upon him like nut-crackers. I threw the bear from me, but the Nareskin remained sprawling, unable to extricate his head from the bear's jaws, imploring for mercy. I gave the wretch his life: a lion preys not upon carcases.

At the same time my troop had effectually routed the bears and the rest of their adversaries. I was merciful, and ordered quarter to be given.

At that moment I perceived Wauwau flying at a great height through the heavens, and we instantly set out in pursuit of her, and never stopped until we arrived at Kamschatka; thence we passed to Otaheite. I met my old acquaintance Omai, who had been in England with the great navigator, Cook, and I was glad to find he had established Sunday schools over all the islands. I talked to him of Europe, and his former voyage to England. 'Ah!' he said, most emphatically, 'the English, the cruel English, to murder me with goodness, and refine upon my torture—took me to Europe, and showed me the court of England, the delicacy of exquisite life: they showed me gods, and showed me heaven, as if on purpose to make me feel the loss of them.'

From these islands we set out, attended by a fleet of canoes with fighting-stages and the chiefest warriors of the islands, commanded by Omai. Thus the chariot of Queen Mab, my team of bulls and the crickets, the ark, the Sphinx, and the balloons, with Hilaro Frosticos, Gog and Magog, Lord Whittington, and the Lord Mayor's show, Don Quixote, &c., with my fleet of canoes, altogether cut a very formidable appearance on our arrival at the Isthmus of Darien. Sensible of what general benefit it would be to mankind, I immediately formed a plan of cutting a canal across the isthmus from sea to sea.

For this purpose I drove my chariot with the greatest impetuosity repeatedly from shore to shore, in the same track, tearing up the rocks and earth thereby, and forming a tolerable bed for the water. Gog and Magog next advanced at the head of a million of people from the realms of North and South America, and from Europe, and with infinite labour cleared away the earth, &c., that I had ploughed up with my chariot. I then again drove my chariot, making the canal wider and deeper, and ordered Gog and Magog to repeat their labour as before. The canal being a quarter of a mile broad, and three hundred yards in depth, I thought it sufficient, and immediately let in the waters of the sea. I did imagine, that from the rotatory motion of the earth on its axis from west to east the sea would be higher on the eastern than the western coast, and that on the uniting of the two seas there would be a strong current from the east, and it happened just as I expected. The sea came in with tremendous magnificence, and enlarged the bounds of the canal, so as to make a passage of some miles broad from ocean to ocean, and make an island of South America. Several sail of trading vessels and men-of-war sailed through this new channel to the South Seas, China, &c., and saluted me with all their cannon as they passed.

I looked through my telescope at the moon, and perceived the philosophers there in great commotion. They could plainly discern the alteration on the surface of our globe, and thought themselves somehow interested in the enterprise of their fellow-mortals in a neighbouring planet. They seemed to think it admirable that such little beings as we men should attempt so magnificent a performance, that would be observable even in a separate world.

Thus having wedded the Atlantic Ocean to the South Sea, I returned to England, and found Wauwau precisely in the very spot whence she had set out, after having led us a chase all round the world.

CHAPTER XIII

The Baron goes to Petersburgh, and converses with the Empress—Persuades the Russians and Turks to cease cutting one another's throats, and in concert cut a canal across the Isthmus of Suez—The Baron discovers the Alexandrine Library, and meets with Hermes Trismegistus—Besieges Seringapatam, and challenges Tippoo Saib to single combat—They fight—The Baron receives some wounds on his face, but at last vanquishes the tyrant—The Baron returns to Europe, and raises the hull of the Royal George

Seized with a fury of canal-cutting, I took it in my head to form an immediate communication between the Mediterranean and the Red Sea, and therefore set out for Petersburgh.

The sanguinary ambition of the Empress would not listen to my proposals, until I took a private opportunity, taking a cup of coffee with her Majesty, to tell her that I would absolutely sacrifice myself for the general good of mankind, and if she would accede to my proposals, would, on the completion of the canal, *ipso facto*, give her my hand in marriage!

'My dear, dear Baron,' said she, 'I accede to everything you please, and agree to make peace with the Porte on the conditions you mention. And,' added she, rising with all the majesty of the Czarina, Empress of half the world, 'be it known to all subjects, that We ordain these conditions, for such is our royal will and pleasure.'

I now proceeded to the Isthmus of Suez, at the head of a million of Russian pioneers, and there united my forces with a million of Turks, armed with shovels and pickaxes. They did not come to cut each other's throats, but for their mutual interest, to facilitate commerce and civilization, and pour all the wealth of India by a new channel into Europe. 'My brave fellows,' said I, 'consider the immense labour of the Chinese to build their celebrated wall; think of what superior benefit to mankind is our present undertaking; persevere, and fortune will second your endeavours. Remember it is Munchausen who leads you on, and be convinced of success.'

Saying these words, I drove my chariot with all my might in my former track, that vestige mentioned by the Baron de Tott, and when I was advanced considerably, I felt my chariot sinking under me. I attempted to drive on, but the ground, or rather immense vault, giving way, my chariot and all went down precipitately. Stunned by the fall, I was some moments before I could recollect myself, when at length, to my amaze-

ment, I perceived myself fallen into the Alexandrine Library, overwhelmed in an ocean of books; thousands of volumes came tumbling on my head amidst the ruins of that part of the vault through which my chariot had descended, and for a time buried my bulls and all beneath a heap of learning. However, I contrived to extricate myself, and advanced with awful admiration through the vast avenues of the library. I perceived on every side innumerable volumes and repositories of ancient learning, and all the science of the Antediluvian world. Here I met with Hermes Trismegistus, and a parcel of old philosophers debating upon the politics and learning of their days. I gave them inexpressible delight in telling them, in a few words, all the discoveries of Newton, and the history of the world since their time. These gentry, on the contrary, told me a thousand stories of antiquity that some of our antiquarians would give their very eyes to hear.

In short, I ordered the library to be preserved, and I intend making a present of it, as soon as it arrives in England, to the Royal Society, together with Hermes Trismegistus, and half a dozen old philosophers. I have got a beautiful cage made, in which I keep these extraordinary creatures, and feed them with bread and honey, as they seem to believe in a kind of doctrine of transmigration, and will not touch flesh. Hermes Trismegistus especially is a most antique looking being, with a beard half a yard long, covered with a robe of golden embroidery, and prates like a parrot. He will cut a very brilliant figure in the Museum.

Having made a track with my chariot from sea to sea, I ordered my Turks and Russians to begin, and in a few hours we had the pleasure of seeing a fleet of British East Indiamen in full sail through the canal. The officers of this fleet were

very polite, and paid me every applause and congratulation my exploits could merit. They told me of their affairs in India, and the ferocity of that dreadful warrior, Tippoo Saib, on which I resolved to go to India and encounter the tyrant. I travelled down the Red Sea to Madras, and at the head of a few Sepoys and Europeans pursued the flying army of Tippoo to the gates of Seringapatam. I challenged him to mortal combat, and, mounted on my steed, rode up to the walls of the fortress amidst a storm of shells and cannon balls. As fast as the bombs and cannon-balls came upon me, I caught them in my hands like so many pebbles, and throwing them against the fortress, demolished the strongest ramparts of the place. I took my mark so direct, that whenever I aimed a cannon-ball or a shell at any person on the ramparts I was sure to hit him:

and one time perceiving a tremendous piece of artillery pointed against me, and knowing the ball must be so great it would certainly stun me, I took a small cannon-ball, and just as I perceived the engineer going to order them to fire, and opening his mouth to give the word of command, I took aim and drove my ball precisely down his throat.

Tippoo, fearing that all would be lost, that a general and successful storm would ensue if I continued to batter the place, came forth upon his elephant to fight me; I saluted him, and insisted he should fire first.

Tippoo, though a barbarian, was not deficient in politeness, and declined the compliment; upon which I took off my hat, and bowing, told him it was an advantage Munchausen should never be said to accept from so gallant a warrior: on which Tippoo instantly discharged his carbine, the ball from which, hitting my horse's ear, made him plunge with rage and indignation. In return I discharged my pistol at Tippoo and shot off his turban. He had a small field-piece mounted with him on his elephant, which he then discharged at me, and the grape-shot coming in a shower, rattled in the laurels that covered and shaded me all over, and remained pendant like berries on the branches. I then advancing, took the proboscis of his elephant, and turning it against the rider, struck him repeatedly with the extremity of it on either side of the head, until I at length dismounted him. Nothing could equal the rage of the barbarian finding himself thrown from his elephant. He rose in a fit of despair, and rushed against my steed and myself: but I scorned to fight him at so great a disadvantage on his side, and directly dismounted to fight him hand to hand. Never did I fight with any man who bore himself more nobly than this adversary; he parried my blows, and dealt

home his own in return with astonishing precision. The first blow of his sabre I received upon the bridge of my nose, and but for the bony firmness of that part of my face, it would have descended to my mouth. I still bear the mark upon my nose.

He next made a furious blow at my head, but I, parrying, deadened the force of his sabre, so that I received but one scar on my forehead, and at the same instant, by a blow of my sword, cut off his arm, and his hand and sabre fell to the earth; he tottered for some paces, and dropped at the foot of his elephant. That sagacious animal, seeing the danger of his master, endeavoured to protect him by flourishing his proboscis round the head of the Sultan.

Fearless I advanced against the elephant, desirous to take alive the haughty Tippoo Saib; but he drew a pistol from his belt, and discharged it full in my face as I rushed upon him, which did me no further harm than wound my cheek-bone, which disfigures me somewhat under my left eye. I could not withstand the rage and impulse of that moment, and with one blow of my sword separated his head from his body.

I returned overland from India to Europe with admirable velocity, so that the account of Tippoo's defeat by me has not as yet arrived by the ordinary passage, nor can you expect to hear of it for a considerable time. I simply relate the encounter as it happened between the Sultan and me; and if there be any one who doubts the truth of what I say, he is an infidel, and I will fight him at any time and place, and with any weapon he pleases.

Hearing so many persons talk about raising the Royal George, I began to take pity on that fine old ruin of British plank, and determined to have her up. I was sensible of the failure of the various means hitherto employed for the purpose, and therefore inclined to try a method different from any before attempted. I got an immense balloon, made of the toughest sail-cloth, and having descended in my diving-bell, and properly secured the hull with enormous cables, I ascended to the surface, and fastened my cables to the balloon. Prodigious multitudes were assembled to behold the elevation of the Royal George, and as soon as I began to fill my balloon with inflammable air the vessel evidently began to move: but when my balloon was completely filled, she carried up the Royal George with the greatest rapidity. The vessel appearing on the surface occasioned a universal shout of triumph from the millions assembled on the occasion. Still the balloon continued ascending, trailing the hull after like a lantern at the tail of a kite, and in a few minutes appeared floating among the clouds.

It was then the opinion of many philosophers that it would be more difficult to get her down than it had been to draw her up. But I convinced them to the contrary by taking my aim so exactly with a twelve-pounder, that I brought her down in an instant.

I considered, that if I should break the balloon with a cannon-ball while she remained with the vessel over the land, the fall would inevitably occasion the destruction of the hull, and which, in its fall, might crush some of the multitude; therefore I thought it safer to take my aim when the balloon was over the sea, and pointing my twelve-pounder, drove the ball right through the balloon, on which the inflammable air rushed out with great force, and the Royal George descended like a falling star into the very spot from whence she had been taken. There she still remains, and I have convinced all Europe of the possibility of taking her up.

CHAPTER XIV

*The Baron makes a speech to the National Assembly,
and drives out all the members—Routs the fishwomen
and the National Guards—Pursues the whole rout into a
Church, where he defeats the National Assembly, &c.,
with Rousseau, Voltaire, and Beelzebub at their head,
and liberates Marie Antoinette and the Royal Family*

Passing through Switzerland on my return from India, I was informed that several of the German nobility had been deprived of the honours and immunities of their French estates. I heard of the sufferings of the amiable Marie Antoinette, and swore to avenge every look that had threatened her with insult. I went to the cavern of these Anthropophagi, assembled to debate, and gracefully putting the hilt of my sword to my lips—'I swear,' cried I, 'by the sacred cross of my sword, that if you do not instantly reinstate your king and his nobility, and your injured queen, I will cut the one half of you to pieces.'

On which the President, taking up a leaden inkstand, flung it at my head. I stooped to avoid the blow, and rushing to the tribunal seized the Speaker, who was fulminating against the Aristocrats, and taking the creature by one leg, flung him at the President. I laid about me most nobly, drove them all out of the house, and locking the doors put the key in my pocket.

I then went to the poor king, and making my obeisance to him—'Sire,' said I, 'your enemies have all fled. I alone am the National Assembly at present, and I shall register your edicts to recall the princes and the nobility; and in future, if your majesty pleases, I will be your Parliament and Council.' He thanked me, and the amiable Marie Antoinette, smiling, gave me her hand to kiss.

At that moment I perceived a party of the National Assembly, who had rallied with the National Guards, and a vast procession of fishwomen, advancing against me. I deposited their Majesties in a place of safety, and with my drawn sword advanced against my foes. Three hundred fishwomen, with bushes dressed with ribbons in their hands, came hallowing and roaring against me like so many furies. I scorned to defile my sword with their blood, but seized the first that came up, and making her kneel down I knighted her with my sword, which so terrified the rest that they all set up a frightful yell and ran away as fast as they could for fear of being aristo-crated by knighthood.

As to the National Guards and the rest of the Assembly, I soon put them to flight; and having made prisoners of some of them, compelled them to take down their national, and put the old royal cockade in its place.

I then pursued the enemy to the top of a hill, where a most noble edifice dazzled my sight; noble and sacred it was, but now converted to the vilest purposes, their monument *de grands hommes*, a Christian church that these Saracens had per-verted into abomination. I burst open the doors, and entered sword in hand. Here I observed all the National Assembly marching round a great altar erected to Voltaire; there was his statue in triumph, and the fishwomen with garlands deck-ing it, and singing 'Ça ira!' I could bear the sight no longer; but rushed upon these pagans, and sacrificed them by dozens on the spot. The members of the Assembly, and the fish-women, continued to invoke their great Voltaire, and all their masters in this monument *de grands hommes*, imploring them to come down and succour them against the Aristocrats and the sword of Munchausen. Their cries were horrible, like the shrieks of witches and enchanters versed in magic and the black art, while the thunder growled, and storms shook the battlements, and Rousseau, Voltaire and Beelzebub appeared, three horrible spectres; one all meagre, mere skin and bone, and cadaverous, seemed death, that hideous skeleton; it was Voltaire, and in his hand were a lyre and a dagger. On the other side was Rousseau, with a chalice of sweet poison in his hand, and between them was their father Beelzebub!

I shuddered at the sight, and with all the enthusiasm of rage, horror, and piety, rushed in among them. I seized that cursed skeleton Voltaire, and soon compelled him to renounce all the errors he had advanced; and while he spoke the words, as if by magic charm, the whole assembly shrieked, and their pandemonium began to tumble in hideous ruin on their heads.

I returned in triumph to the palace, where the Queen rushed into my arms, weeping tenderly. 'Ah, thou flower of nobility,' cried she, 'were all the nobles of France like thee, we should never have been brought to this!'

I bade the lovely creature dry her eyes, and with the King and Dauphin ascend my carriage, and drive post to Mont-Medi, as not an instant was to be lost. They took my advice and drove away. I conveyed them within a few miles of Mont-Medi, when the King, thanking me for my assistance, hoped I would not trouble myself any farther, as he was then, he presumed, out of danger; and the Queen also, with tears in her eyes, thanked me on her knees, and presented the Dauphin for my blessing. In short, I left the King eating a mutton chop. I advised him not to delay, or he would certainly be taken, and setting spurs to my horse, wished them a good evening, and returned to England. If the King remained too long at table, and was taken, it was not my fault.

THE EARLY EDITIONS OF
MUNCHAUSEN'S TRAVELS

It would be a useless, probably an impossible task to compile a bibliography of an uncopyrighted classic which at one time or another has attracted the attention of unnumbered publishers and jobbing printers, each copying the mistakes of his predecessor. There is, however, room for what with some hesitation I have attempted—a record of the first fourteen years of the book's European existence. Even in so limited a field as this (which excludes several very early American editions, as well as the fine editions of the nineteenth century) there may well be lurking pirates whom I have neglected.

The main purposes of this bibliographical record are, however, well served by using 1800 as a limiting date. It is the great rarity of the earliest editions that makes the unravelling of their history worth while; fourteen years are enough to show how the titles swell from the modest solo of the First Edition to the pompous chorus of the Eighth; by deploying the editions published in those years the haphazard growth of the canon can be illustrated and the method used in establishing the text of the present edition justified.

Of the editions in this chosen field all that I have been able to trace are listed below. I have recorded in some detail such copies of the earliest editions as I have been able to locate, and have given collations of the first three English editions. This I have supplemented in most cases by a more general note on the textual peculiarities of the edition in question and the use that has been made of it in preparing the present text.

I owe it to many collectors and librarians that I can claim to have examined personally copies of most of the books described. Where this has not been possible, I am equally indebted for transcribed particulars. I should especially acknowledge the kindness of Mr E. Hubert Litchfield, of New York, for allowing me to examine his unique collection of Munchausens, which includes the First, Third and 'Third' editions. I am also in debt to Professor W. A. Jackson of the Houghton Library at Harvard, to Mr H. R. Mead of the Huntington Library, and to Mr S. I. Grinberg of the Saltykov-Shchedrin State Public Library, Leningrad, for particulars of three of the four recorded copies of the true Second Edition; to Major-General C. E. Edward-Collins for particulars of the very uncommon 'Fourth' Edition in his possession; and to Mr D. J. Cameron for details of his almost equally uncommon 'Sixth' Edition; also to Mr G. Allen Hutt, for a valuable draught from his deep knowledge of Russica; and to Mr John Hayward for his wholly indispensable advice and encouragement.   J. C.

BIBLIOGRAPHY

NOTE: *The establishment of III below as the true Second Edition displaces the traditional order of the editions which follow, and their imprints cannot, therefore, be accepted at their face value. Justice demands that IV below, which lays claim only to be 'A New Edition', should now receive its rightful title of Third; but I have thought it reasonable to deal with the other masqueraders by placing quotation marks round their old titles to show that they may hold them only by courtesy. It is important that the reader should remember this when distinguishing between the Third and 'Third' editions.*

I

VADE MECUM FÜR LUSTIGE LEUTE. *Mylius.* BERLIN. Number VIII (1781) and Number X (1783).

The first of these contains 'M-H-SCHE GESCHICHTEN' (sixteen anecdotes), and the second 'NOCH ZWEI M- LÜGEN'. All the eighteen anecdotes are reprinted in the authoritative edition of Bürger's *Munchausen* edited by Erich Ebstein and published by the *Gesellschaft der Bibliophilen*. Weimar. 1925.

These anecdotes and their authorship are discussed in the Introduction. Fifteen of the first sixteen, and both the other two are used in the First Edition (II below).

II

FIRST EDITION

BARON MUNCHAUSEN'S NARRATIVE OF HIS MARVELLOUS TRAVELS AND CAMPAIGNS IN RUSSIA. HUMBLY DEDICATED AND RECOMMENDED TO COUNTRY GENTLEMEN; AND, IF THEY PLEASE, to be repeated as their own, after a Hunt, at Horse Races, in Watering Places, and other such polite Assemblies, round the bottle and fireside. OXFORD:

Printed for the Editor and sold by the Booksellers there and at Cambridge, also in London by the Booksellers of Piccadilly, the Royal Exchange, and M. Smith, at No. 46, in Fleet-Street. MDCCLXXXVI. *Price One Shilling.*

12mo (in half-sheets). The British Museum copy collates: [A] four leaves, B–E⁶ (E5ᵛ blank: E6 blank and genuine), consisting of half-title [A1], title [A2] with five *errata* listed on verso, Preface pp. i–iv [A3] and [A4], and text pp [5]–49 followed by a blank leaf [E6].

The title-page in this edition is post-dated 1786 in accordance with a practice then common: the book actually seems to have appeared late in 1785, being noticed in the *Gentleman's Magazine* and *Critical Review* for December of that year, but no copies bearing the date 1785 are recorded, and there is no reason for supposing that any ever existed.

Of the three copies which can be traced, one, the finest, is in the library of E. Hubert Litchfield of New York; a second was sold at the Parke-Bernet Galleries in New York in the 'United Features' Sale in 1937. The third, bound in with other pamphlets, is in the British Museum. I have been unable to locate the Hibbert copy (sprinkled calf, g.e. by Bedford; sold Sotheby's, April 11th, 1902). It may be the same copy as that sold in the 'United Features' Sale.

The narrative given in the First Edition has been skilfully constructed (almost certainly by Raspe) from the *Vade Mecum* anecdotes, and is here reprinted from the British Museum copy, reappearing, I believe, for the first time since 1786.

III

SECOND EDITION

Title as in II above, except for the words, *And in Dublin by P. Byrne, No.* 108 *Grafton-Street* added to the imprint. 12mo (in half-sheets. Collation as in II above. There is no list of *errata*, four of the five *errata* listed in the First Edition being corrected in the text.

Four copies are recorded. One, formerly in the Church collection, is now in the Huntington Library; a second, lacking the half-title, is in the Houghton Library at Harvard. Through the good offices of the Society for Cultural Relations with the U.S.S.R., the Librarian of the Saltykov-Shchedrin State Public Library, Leningrad, has supplied details of a third copy. These three copies are in the original printed paper wrappers (the Church-Huntington copy, however, lacking the upper cover). A fourth copy—White-Hogan—lacking the wrappers, the half-title and final blank, was sold in 1946 at the Parke-Bernet Galleries, New York. (Cohen Sale Catalogue, lot 456.)

Although the text is that of the First Edition, this edition, with the Dublin imprint, was reset and is not a re-issue. The text, which for the establishment of readings is not very valuable, is marred by numerous misprints which do not appear in the earlier edition (e.g. 'freightened' for 'frightened', etc.).

IV

THIRD EDITION

SINGULAR TRAVELS, CAMPAIGNS, VOYAGES, AND SPORTING ADVENTURES OF BARON MUNNIKHOUSON, COMMONLY PRONOUNCED MUNCHAUSEN; AS HE RELATES THEM OVER A BOTTLE WHEN SURROUNDED BY HIS FRIENDS. A New Edition, considerably enlarged, and ornamented with four Views, engraved from the Baron's own Drawings. OXFORD: *Printed and sold by the Booksellers of that University, and at Cambridge, Bath and Bristol; and in London by M. Smith, at No. 46 Fleet-Street; and by the Booksellers in Paternoster Row*, 1786.

12mo (in half-sheets). The Litchfield copy collates A–H^6 consisting of half-title, title, Prefaces A3-A6 (verso blank). Text B1-H3 followed by Contents H4-H6 (verso blank). One *erratum* is printed at the foot of H6^r. Four inserted engravings on one side of a single folding sheet, signed 'Munchausen pinxit', and dated, as is also the 'Advertisement to the Second Edition', April 20th, 1786.

This traditionally ranks as the Second Edition, but the establishment of III above must displace it to Third. The only copy which I have been able to locate is in the collection of E. Hubert Litchfield, New York. Another copy is recorded in the Göttingen University Library, but inquiries made on the spot by a colleague recently working there have failed to trace it.

The text of this edition adds five new stories ('The Naval Adventures') to the narrative of the first two editions. These stories, which seem to be Raspe's work, form the second section of the present reprint. It is just possible that the four illustrations are also from Raspe's pencil—we know that he prided himself on his draughtsmanship and did in fact illustrate some of his scientific and antiquarian works.

V

'THIRD' EDITION

GULLIVER REVIVED, OR THE SINGULAR TRAVELS, CAMPAIGNS, VOYAGES, AND ADVENTURES OF BARON MUNIKHOUSON, COMMONLY CALLED MUNCHAUSEN. The Third Edition, considerably enlarged, and ornamented with a number of Views, engraved from the original Designs. OXFORD: *Printed for the Editor and sold by G. Kearsley at No. 46 in Fleet-Street, 1786. Entered at Stationers Hall.*

[The half-title reads: Gulliver Revived (Price Two Shillings). Entered at Stationers-Hall.]

12mo (in half-sheets). 156 pp. Sixteen inserted engravings, the original four on one side of a single folding sheet, the twelve new ones individually inserted and bearing the date May 26th, 1786. The prefatory 'Note to the Third Edition' is dated May 18th, 1786. There is a copy in the Bodleian and another in the original boards in the possession of E. Hubert Litchfield, New York.

Although, from his address, there is reason to suppose that Kearsley had always had an interest in Munchausen, this edition is the first to bear his ostensible imprint, and it was probably at this stage that Munchausen left Raspe's hands. The new edition, with its more profuse illustrations and doubled price, was clearly intended for a more genteel public, and it was presumably for such readers that the extensive revision of the text was carried out which has corrupted most subsequent reprints. The fresh matter (which is here printed in the third section) is the work of a different and less talented hand than Raspe's. A peculiar feature of this edition is a detailed Contents headed 'Heads of the Established Facts' placed at the end of the book. The idea may have come from the German Edition (VI below) which appeared at about the same time.

VI

FIRST GERMAN EDITION

WUNDERBARE REISEN ZU WASSER UND LANDE, FELDZÜGE UND LUSTIGE ABENTHEUER DES FREYHERRN VON MÜNCHHAUSEN WIE ER DIESELBEN BEY DER FLASCHE IM ZIRKEL SEINER FREUNDE ZU ERZÄHLEN PFLEGT. Aus dem Englischen nach der neuesten Ausgabe übersetzt, hier und da erweitert und mit noch mehr Küpfern gezieret. LONDON, 1786.

12mo. vi+114 pp. Seven inserted engravings of which three are original and four taken from the Third Edition, but re-cut and reversed in piratical fashion. There is a fine copy in the British Museum, but even in Germany copies are extremely uncommon.

This edition bears a false imprint, having in fact been published in Göttingen by Johann Christian Dieterich: it may actually have appeared before V above, as the text is a free translation, with considerable embellishment, by Gottfried August Bürger, of the English Third Edition. The German text, which is the archetype of continental Munchausens, has been reprinted by the *Gesellschaft der Bibliophilen* (cf. I above).

VII

'FOURTH' EDITION

GULLIVER REVIVED CONTAINING SINGULAR TRAVELS, CAMPAIGNS, VOYAGES, AND ADVENTURES IN RUSSIA, ICELAND, TURKEY, EGYPT, GIBRALTAR, UP THE MEDITERRANEAN, AND ON THE ATLANTIC OCEAN: Also an Account of a Voyage into the MOON, with many extraordinary Particulars relative to the Cooking Animal in that Planet, which are here called the Human Species, BY BARON MUNCHAUSEN. The Fourth Edition. Considerably enlarged, and ornamented with Sixteen explanatory Views, engraved from Original Designs. LONDON: *Printed for G. Kearsley, in Fleet-Street.* MDCCLXXXVI. *Price Half a Crown. Entered at Stationers-Hall.*

12mo. 172 pp. Eighteen (not sixteen) inserted engravings (some on folding sheets) including a folding frontispiece illustrating the Voyage to the Moon. The 'Preface to the Fourth Edition' is dated July 12th, 1786. I owe the description of this rare edition to Major General C. E. Edward-Collins, from the copy in his possession. I have been unable to trace another.

This edition follows the revised text, which first appeared in the 'Third' Edition, in every respect save in the de Tott story, for which a version is given which rather resembles the original form printed in the Third Edition (IV above). Considerable new accretions include the Baron's journey by cannon fire, the voyage with Captain Hamilton, and (as a supplement) the Trip to the Moon. I have grouped all these in the fourth section of the present text.

Subsequent reprints, including that made by Mr Harvey Darton for the Navarre Society in 1931 'from the earliest editions', have treated this or later editions, with their debased text, as authoritative. How little it is deserving of this respect (except for the stories which appear in it for the first time) can be judged from the boast in the preface that it may be considered as almost 'a new work'. Among the many activities of the editor was the suppression of the 'round the bottle and fireside' fiction, and the reduction of the now unwieldy continuous narrative into chapters.

VIII

'FIFTH' EDITION

GULLIVER REVIVED, CONTAINING SINGULAR TRAVELS, CAMPAIGNS, VOYAGES, AND ADVENTURES IN RUSSIA, THE CASPIAN SEA, ICELAND, TURKEY, EGYPT, GIBRALTAR, UP THE MEDITERRANEAN, ON THE ATLANTIC OCEAN AND THROUGH THE CENTRE OF MOUNT ETNA INTO THE SOUTH SEA: Also an Account of a Voyage to the MOON and DOG STAR, with many extraordinary Particulars relative to the Cooking Animal in those Planets, which are here called the Human Species, by BARON MUNCHAUSEN. The Fifth Edition, considerably enlarged, and ornamented with a variety of explanatory Views, engraved from Original Designs. LONDON: *Printed for G. Kearsley, in Fleet-Street.* MDCCLXXXVII.

12mo (in half-sheets). xxiv + 208 pp. Nineteen inserted engravings variously dated, some on folding sheets, including a new frontispiece dated December 23rd, 1786. The 'Preface to the Fourth Edition' appears with the new date November 22nd, 1786. This is the commonest of the seven earliest English editions. The two advertisements (A6^v and K4^v): (i) for a book on astrology and (ii) for a book of mediaeval tales on which 'The principal part of our romances and dramatic pieces have been founded', indicate the turn public fancy was taking and the special interests of Munchausen's publisher.

The text follows that of the 'Fourth' edition and adds two new chapters, one (the Voyage to Ceylon) being placed at the beginning, and the other (the Descent into Mount Etna) at the end: they have been printed here in the fourth section with the other late accretions. The twenty chapters of this edition make up what is usually printed as the 'First Part of the Baron's Travels'.

IX

FIRST FRENCH EDITION

GULLIVER RESSUSCITÉ, OU LES VOYAGES, CAMPAGNES ET AVENTURES EXTRAORDINAIRES DU BARON DE MUNIKHOUSON. PARIS: *Chez Royez, Libraire, Quai des Agustins.* MDCCLXXXVII.

12mo. 96 pp. No illustrations. There is a copy in the British Museum.

The text, with minor variations, possibly to suit the censorship, is a translation of that given in the English 'Fifth' edition (VIII above), but is divided into two parts, each with its own title page, and not into chapters.

X

SECOND GERMAN EDITION

WUNDERBARE REISEN ZU WASSER UND LANDE, FELDZÜGE UND LUSTIGE ABENTHEUER DES FREYHERRN VON MÜNCHHAUSEN, WIE ER DIESELBEN BEY DER FLASCHE IM ZIRKEL SEINER FREUNDE ZU ERZÄHLEN PFLEGT. Aus dem Englischen nach der neuesten Ausgabe übersetzt und mit noch mehr Küpfern gezieret. Zweite vermehrte Ausgabe. LONDON, 1788.

12mo. 176 pp. 16 inserted engravings.

This edition, like its predecessor, bears a false imprint, concealing the identity of Dieterich, of Göttingen. The text of the First German edition is here expanded with a translation of the new matter included in the 'Fifth' English edition. Bürger's editing was, however, extensive, and it may be said that it is from this edition onwards that the English and Continental Munchausens follow different paths.

XI

'SIXTH' EDITION

GULLIVER REVIVED OR THE VICE OF LYING PROPERLY EXPOSED; CONTAINING SINGULAR TRAVELS, CAMPAIGNS, VOYAGES, AND ADVENTURES IN RUSSIA, THE CASPIAN SEA, ICELAND, TURKEY, EGYPT, GIBRALTAR, UP THE MEDITERRANEAN, ON THE ATLANTIC OCEAN AND THROUGH THE CENTRE OF MOUNT ETNA INTO THE SOUTH SEA: also an Account of a Voyage into the MOON and DOG-STAR with many extraordinary Particulars relative to the Cooking Animal in those Planets, which are there called the Human Species by BARON MUNCHAUSEN. The Sixth Edition.

Considerably enlarged and ornamented with a variety of explanatory Views engraved from Original Designs. LONDON: *Printed for G. Kearsley, in Fleet-Street*. MDCCLXXXIX.

12mo. 252 pp+10 pp. of inserted advertisements at the end. 20 inserted engravings (as in VIII above with a new frontispiece). Only two copies located (1) Huntington Library; (2) D. J. Cameron, Birmingham.

This uncommon edition adds the 'Journey on the Eagle's Back' to the text printed in the 'Fifth' edition. It is this story—usually printed (as it first appeared) under the title of *Supplement*—which I have here inserted as the last part of the fourth section. It probably comes from the same pens (not Raspe's) as the rest of the contents of that section.

XII

PIRATED 'SIXTH' EDITION

Title as for 'Fifth' Edition, with the addition: 'A new Edition, considerably enlarged, and ornamented with beautiful copper plates. HAMBURGH: *B. G. Hoffmann*. 1790'.

12mo. 19 inserted engravings (copied from the 'Fifth' Edition) and text, with minor variants, from the 'Sixth' Edition.

XIII

FIRST EDITION OF THE *SEQUEL*

A SEQUEL TO THE ADVENTURES OF BARON MUNCHAUSEN HUMBLY DEDICATED TO MR BRUCE THE ABYSSINIAN TRAVELLER, As the Baron conceives that it may be of some service to him making another expedition into Abyssinia; but if this does not delight Mr Bruce, the Baron is willing to fight him on any terms he pleases. [LONDON:] *Printed for H. D. Symonds, Paternoster Row*, November 1st. 1792.

12mo. 240 pp. 20 inserted engravings.

This was a new, and in the first instance competing work, though an accommodation seems soon to have been reached between Kearsley and Symonds by which the *Sequel* became 'Volume Two of the Baron's Travels'. It is often so reprinted. The original travels are advertised in the *Sequel*. I have reprinted the *Sequel* as the fifth section in the present text.

XIV

'SEVENTH' EDITION

The SEVENTH EDITION, Considerably enlarged, and ornamented with Twenty Explanatory Engravings, from Original Designs. GULLIVER REVIVED: OR, THE VICE OF LYING PROPERLY EXPOSED. CONTAINING SINGULAR TRAVELS, CAMPAIGNS, VOYAGES, AND ADVENTURES IN RUSSIA, THE CASPIAN SEA, ICELAND, TURKEY, EGYPT, GIBRALTAR, UP THE MEDITERRANEAN, ON THE ATLANTIC OCEAN, AND THROUGH THE CENTRE OF MOUNT AETNA, INTO THE SOUTH SEA. ALSO, An Account of a Voyage into the MOON and DOG-STAR; with many extraordinary Particulars relative to the Cooking Animal in those Planets, which are there called the Human Species. BY BARON MUNCHAUSEN. LONDON: *Printed for C. and G. Kearsley, Fleet-Street.* M.DCC.XCIII.

12mo. 264 pp. Twenty inserted engravings, some on folding sheets. The half-title [A1] has an advertisement of the *Sequel* on verso and another advertisement is printed at the end [V6ᵛ]. The 'Preface to the Seventh Edition', which makes the unjustified claim that this edition contains fresh matter, is dated October 16th, 1792. In fact the text of this edition is precisely the same as that of the 'Sixth'. The half-title shows that the price was three shillings and sixpence.

XV

SECOND EDITION OF THE *SEQUEL*

This is a re-issue of the 1792 edition of the *Sequel* (XIII above) with a cancel title-page bearing the date 1796 and the additional words: 'The Second Edition'.

Both issues of the *Sequel*, and particularly the second, are extremely uncommon in isolation, being usually found bound in with the 'Seventh' or 'Eighth' Editions of the earlier work. It may be that this re-issue was not sold separately.

XVI

'EIGHTH' EDITION

Title (except for the date 1799 and 'Eighth' for 'Seventh') and text as for 'Seventh' Edition.

12mo. iv + 200 pp. 20 inserted engravings as in XIV above.

I have thought it best to stop with the turn of the century, for otherwise, though it would include many fascinating and scarce volumes, the tale would be endless. I think it may be said that every one of the books listed above can claim the title 'scarce', while the earliest are certainly 'rare'. Kearsley and Symonds soon lost their monopoly: but it is a strange fact that in an undated reprint, which can scarcely be earlier than 1850, are inserted Symonds's old illustrations to the *Sequel*, taken from the same, and now much worn plates, more than half a century after they were first cut.